ROSES ARE DEAD

A TWIN SISTERS COZY MYSTERY

AMY GRUNDY

Roses Are Dead
A Twin Sisters Cozy Mystery - Book 1
By Amy Grundy

ISBN - 978-1-952392-21-4

 Created with Vellum

ACKNOWLEDGMENTS

Special thanks to my beta readers, Jeff Lendermon, Beth Fitz, Monica Mondrik and Robert Fuller. I always appreciate the time you spend reading my books and your invaluable input.

Cover art created by Molly Burton – Thank you so much for these intriguing covers. I hope my story does your cover justice.

COZY COVER DESIGNS

This book is dedicated to all the seniors out there with a zest for life. Keep on keeping on.

CHAPTER ONE

"SAY NO TO CONDOS! Say no to condos!"

"Say no to condos! Say no to condos!"

The chanting from the crowds on the sidewalk got Iris's attention even though the windows of her old Subaru were closed. Iris Abernathy watched as the traffic crept down Main Street. A small crowd was now gathered in front of City Hall, with people waving their picket signs. Blue Water Bay was such a small quiet town, at least it had been the last time she visited here. What in the world was going on? The light changed to red, allowing time for her to get a good look at the crowd. They continued to chant and a petite young brunette walked up and down the sidewalk handing out flyers to people as they passed by.

A smartly dressed young man approached the crowd and the dark-haired woman stopped in her tracks, staring at him. His lip curled in a sneer as he shook his head. "You can't stop me," he yelled above the chanting. "This deal will go through."

The woman's face turned a bright shade of red. "Just

watch us," she yelled back, before picking up a sign and waving it in his face. "Say no to condos!"

The honking of a car horn brought Iris's attention back to the light which was now green. She eased into the intersection, thinking how her sister Ivy Mae would definitely be able to give her the scoop on what was going on in town. Half a second later the screeching of tires caused her to jerk her head to the right. There was nothing she could do. The impact rocked Iris in her seat, her hands flew up off the steering wheel, and shards of glass pelted her from the side. Her side-impact airbag prevented her from cracking her head on the side window too hard. Everything was moving in slow motion.

What on earth? That car ran a red light, Iris thought trying to clear her head. She knew she had the green light. About that time, a young man yanked open the driver's side door.

"I'm so sorry. Are you alright?"

"Yes, I think so." Iris stammered, straightening her wire-frame glasses that were hanging off her nose. She gripped the door frame in an attempt to get to her feet. It had been a long drive and her knees creaked as she stood upright. Shards of glass rained down on the pavement as she stood up.

"My Uncle Norman is going to kill me. This is his truck. I'm so sorry, I wasn't looking at the light."

Iris lifted her hand up to the side of her head. "I suppose I should move my car out of the road?"

Charlie walked around Iris's car again, "I'm not sure you're going to be able to do that."

"Why not?" Her steps were shaky, and she kept her hand on the hood of her car as she edged around it. Her voice caught in her throat, "Oh, my goodness, you're right."

Her front right tire was flat and sat at an odd angle to the rest of the car. "I need a wrecker." Iris lowered her hand from her head. Blood spotted her palm. "Oh goodness."

"Here take this." Charlie pulled out a red handkerchief from his pocket and handed it over to Iris.

"Iris, Iris! Are you alright?"

That voice was unmistakable and Iris turned to see her twin sister Ivy Mae hurrying down the sidewalk in her direction. "I just knew something was wrong." Ivy Mae gripped her twin in a fierce hug, then abruptly let her go when Iris winced. "Oh, I'm sorry, are you alright?"

"Oh, now, don't fret. I'm fine or mostly fine. My left shoulder is a bit sore, but I'm sure it's nothing serious."

"Well, you're bleeding. Let me see."

Iris moved the handkerchief away from her forehead. "Look it's barely bleeding."

"It looks like it's more of a scuff." Ivy Mae smoothed Iris's silver bob back in place and plucked a stray square of safety glass out of her hair.

"Good lord, Charlie, what did you do?" The booming voice preceded the appearance of a sheriff as he climbed out from behind the wheel of his patrol car. He clicked the microphone on his radio and requested a tow truck to the scene. "You ran that red light didn't you, Charlie?"

Charlie scowled, thrusting his hands into the pockets of his jeans. "I didn't mean to. It was an accident." Charlie threw a look over his shoulder toward the young dark-haired woman who was handing out the flyers. The car accident had caught everyone's attention including the protestors. Most of them now resumed their marching and started to chant again.

Sheriff George McGuire followed Charlie's gaze to the young woman. "Uh-huh. More like you weren't paying attention. Why don't you just go talk to her sometime, then maybe you can avoid accidents like this." The sheriff turned his attention to Iris. "Ma'am, are you alright?" He paused taking a closer look at the woman, "Iris is that you?"

"Well of course it is," Ivy Mae spoke up. "Why do you think I'm here?"

"Ha!" The sheriff's belly shook from the laugh. "Ivy Mae, do you really want me to answer that?" He turned his attention to Iris, "It's so good to see you again. How long has it been?"

"Too long, but I'm back now. I'm looking forward to the quiet of small-town life. This wasn't how I thought it would start though."

"Welcome back, maybe you can keep Ivy Mae out of trouble," he smirked, throwing a nod in Ivy Mae's direction.

Ivy Mae crossed her arms, "I don't know what you're talking about George McGuire. I am perfectly capable of taking care of myself and I don't get in trouble."

Iris glanced between the sheriff and her sister. "Is there something I need to know about?"

"I think we should get back to the business at hand, don't you Sheriff?" Ivy Mae huffed.

A deputy had shown up to help direct traffic through the intersection.

"Yes, you're right. Iris, do you think you need an ambulance?"

"No, nothing like that. I think if I can just sit down, I'll be fine."

"Iris, are you sure about that?" Ivy Mae put a protective arm around Iris.

"Oh, now sister, don't fuss. I'll be fine."

"Come on over here and let's get you seated at least while I get your information." He opened the back door of his patrol car and Ivy Mae walked her twin sister over to the car.

Iris put a hand up to the left side of her head that was beginning to ache. "My purse is in the car; won't you get it for me?"

Ivy Mae trotted over to retrieve her sister's purse.

"Charlie," the Sheriff barked, "Make yourself useful. Get the luggage out of the car and bring me your driver's license too. By the way, you might want to give your uncle a call, and let him know what happened before he hears it through the grapevine."

Charlie slunk over and did as he was told. The wrecker pulled up to tow Iris's trusty Subaru off. A few minutes later they had insurance information exchanged and a citation issued to Charlie. Sheriff McGuire looked over at the ladies, "Climb in Ivy Mae and I'll give you ladies a ride home."

"Wait, where is my car being taken to?"

"Don't worry Iris. Blue Water Bay only has one auto repair shop that does bodywork. Travis is the guy you'll want to talk to over there. His shop is two streets over. Ivy Mae knows where it is."

A short ride later, the cruiser pulled up in front of Ivy Mae's cottage-style home. It was white with black shutters and a red tin roof. An old worn brick path led to the front door. Boxwoods, hydrangeas, and hostas filled the flower beds around the front of the home.

"Here we go ladies," the sheriff set the luggage on the front porch. He tipped his hat, "Can you get it from here?"

"I'm sure we can sheriff, but don't you want to come in for some tea?"

"No, I better be getting back."

"Well, I understand how busy you must be," Ivy Mae

held the door open for her sister, "But I've got some freshly baked lemon bars."

Sheriff McGuire tipped his hat higher on his head. "Now I wouldn't want to turn down your lemon bars." He picked up the luggage and followed Ivy Mae into the house.

CHAPTER TWO

"JUST DROP those anywhere sheriff and I'll go get the tea."

"And maybe something for my headache," Iris sat quietly at the small dining table right off the kitchen. A moment later she felt tiny paws on her leg. "Well, hello there Daisy. Come on up here." Iris scooped up the little pooch and stroked her soft curly fur.

"Turn on the water...now where did I put those...oh, here you are," Ivy Mae muttered in the kitchen.

"I don't suppose that was the welcome home you anticipated." The sheriff pulled out a chair at the table across from Iris.

"No, it definitely wasn't, but I'm happy to be back." Daisy licked Iris on the chin then curled up in her lap.

"I know it's been a while, but I was sorry to hear about your husband, Robert. Ivy Mae filled me in."

"Thank you, sheriff. It's been almost a year and a half now, but I still miss him. You know you think you've come to terms, but you're never ready to say goodbye to a spouse. You know?"

"I sure couldn't imagine life without my Polly. God bless her. She puts up with me and my crazy schedule."

The teacups clattered as Ivy Mae came in carrying the heavy tray. "How is Polly? I haven't talked to her in a while now. Not since I loaned her my bike and she mistakenly ran it through the petunias in the town square."

"I thought she was going to break her neck riding that thing," the sheriff laughed. "I guess she's too ornery for that."

"Oh, now stop that," Ivy Mae gave the sheriff a playful swat. "You're lucky to have her."

Ivy Mae set a bottle down in front of her sister. "Take a couple of those and here is your tea with lemon, just like you like it. And here's your honey. Oh, I see Daisy has found a friendly lap."

"Thank you, dear. Yes, she's a sweetie." Iris continued to stroke the pup's head.

"Sheriff, don't be shy. Help yourself." Ivy Mae nudged the plate of lemon bars in his direction.

He reached over eagerly for one of the powdered-sugar topped rectangles.

When everyone was settled Iris spoke up. "So, what was going on out there today. Something about condos."

"Heaven help us. I wish that man had never come to Blue Water Bay. He's got everyone all stirred up," Ivy Mae huffed.

"The short version, Iris, is that a land developer wants to purchase some land down by the coast, past the botanical garden. If everything goes as planned, they will be building some condos down that way," the sheriff paused to sip his tea. He preferred coffee, but tea was what he was offered, so no need to be inhospitable.

Ivy Mae could see a frown forming over the rim of her

sister's teacup. "But they can't do that, doesn't that butt up against the wildlife refuge?"

A sigh escaped from the sheriff, "Yep, but there is a small strip of land that has recently come on the market. There's been a fight over it ever since."

"Ivy Mae, these are some of the best lemon bars that you've ever made."

"Well, here then, have another."

The sheriff grinned as he reached for another bar. "Maybe just one for the road." He drained his teacup. "Thank you, ladies, for the tea. I've got to get going. Iris, you take it easy."

"Let me walk you out," Ivy Mae hopped up from her seat. Daisy raised her head for a moment.

"No, I can see myself out. I'll see you ladies later." Sheriff McGuire picked up his hat and headed out.

The sisters heard the door close and Iris blew out a breath. "I hope that car accident wasn't an indication of things to come."

"What?"

"You know, a bad omen."

A bright cackle escaped from Ivy Mae, "Why sister, you don't believe in omens, bad or otherwise."

"But you do," Iris stated.

"Oh now, that's just poppycock." Ivy Mae reached over and squeezed her sister's hand. "I'm so glad you're here."

Iris's eyes sparkled as a smile lit up her face, "I'm happy to be here too. Now my furniture will be here next week. I'm hoping I can find a place to live before then. Did you find me anything?"

"Ah, well, yes I did," Ivy Mae picked up the cup quickly, attempting to avoid the next question.

"That's great. Is it close by?"

"You could say that," Ivy Mae admitted.

"Well, don't hold back. Tell me about it."

"It's a charming little cottage. Two bedrooms, two baths, lovely garden in the back. There is a sunroom that is excellent for bird watching. Easy access into town."

Iris stared at her sister without blinking, "You're talking about this house, aren't you? Ivy Mae, you know I need my own space and you need your own space too."

"Oh, now sister, think of all the fun we could have. How long has it been since we were together?" Daisy raised her head, looking back and forth between the two ladies.

Iris nodded. Now it was her turn to reach over to take her sister's hand, "Too long, sister."

"We are going to have so much fun," Ivy Mae clapped her hands together, "bike riding, hiking, bird watching..."

"Bike riding? Are you kidding me? I haven't been on a bike in over forty years," Iris huffed. "Ha! I'd probably run over whatever petunia's Polly didn't hit."

"Well, you know what they say, you never forget how to ride a bike," Ivy Mae laughed. "And by the way, technically it's a tricycle since it has the third wheel."

"Uh-huh. I'm not sure that matters."

"And speaking about the botanical garden, I know it's been years since you've seen it, but they've expanded it since the last time you were there. It's really quite lovely."

Iris sat quietly for a moment. Her head was hurting, did she miss part of the conversation? Were they talking about the botanical garden?

"And I know you've always wanted to learn to garden. You should take a look in the backyard. I started a little garden back there last spring."

Iris felt like she needed to follow along better. "A

garden sounds wonderful. What kind of vegetables are you growing?"

"Strawberries."

"Ooh, I know how much you love strawberries. Anything else?"

"A blackberry vine on the back fence."

"I see some things haven't changed."

"Whatever are you talking about sister?" Ivy Mae sipped the last of her tea, looking innocent.

"You never were much for vegetables."

"You weren't either! But you're right. I actually thought I'd see how the berries did before I tried anything else."

"I'd love to give gardening a go. We didn't have room for one in the city. And I guess if I'm going to be staying here, I'm going to need to put my furniture in storage."

"Or if there's anything you want here, I can move some of my stuff out or over to Sara's."

"How is our niece doing?"

"She's doing great. She's working hard to get her B&B off the ground. The up side, besides having her here, is I get to see our dear brother a little more often. He still doesn't make it out here as much as I'd like, but what can I say. That's life."

Iris set her empty cup down, "I can't wait to see her."

"Do you feel up to seeing her tonight? We could go out for dinner?"

"I think that would do me a world of good. Let's do it."

"Come on, I'll help you get your luggage upstairs. You can get settled and I'll call Sara."

"Alright Daisy, I've got to get up now." Iris moved the little dog off her lap. She looked around the room, took a deep breath, and smiled. It was good to be here with her sister, especially after all that had happened. She would always love Robert and still missed him every day, but this was like a new start, one that she was ready for.

"Iris, are you coming?" Ivy Mae called out from the hallway.

"Coming!" The steps creaked in the same places they always did, and the banister felt like silk under her right hand.

"Ivy Mae, what happened up here?"

"Oh, don't look in there," Ivy Mae squeaked.

"How could I not look in there, it's the bathroom? What happened?"

"I put up one of Sara's guests and they let the bathtub overflow. I think they were playing with Daisy and just forgot it." Ivy Mae put her hands on her hips and shook her head. "They didn't even say anything when it happened. The flooring just startled to buckle. I just haven't had the time to get the floors redone yet."

"Did you tell Sara?"

"No, she has enough on her plate right now. I was happy to help her out. I'll get new flooring in there eventually." Ivy Mae turned to look at her sister, "Maybe you could help me pick something out."

"I'd be happy to. I'll go unpack while you make your call."

"My call?"

"To Sara. About dinner."

"Oh, right, I'm on it." Ivy Mae hurried back down the stairs. Iris turned to her room, wondering if a guest left the water running in the tub or was it something her sister did. Unfortunately, Ivy Mae seemed a little forgetful these days.

CHAPTER THREE

"I'D LOVE to go to dinner tonight Auntie," Sara responded. "I'll be there to pick you up in a bit."

After a while, Daisy hopped off her little cushion and headed to the front door, bouncing up and down.

"Come on in," Ivy Mae called out.

"Auntie! How did you know it was me and how come you didn't have that door locked?"

"Oh, pish, posh. Who else would be at the door? You're the only one I was expecting."

Sara rolled her eyes, "Auntie, I think there's something wrong with your logic."

"Sara! Look at you."

Sara turned to see Iris coming into the room. "Aunt Iris! Oh, it's been too long."

"I'm happy to see you, my girl," Iris wrapped her arms around her niece and gave her a squeeze.

"Welcome home, Aunt Iris. I'm so happy that you decided to move back. I know it's not the big town you're used to, but I think you're going to really enjoy it here."

"I'm sure I will. So, where are we going for dinner tonight?"

Sara looked back and forth between her two aunts. "I'll leave it up to you two ladies, but I thought about taking you out to Skippers."

"Ohhh, Skippers, I love their fried shrimp and fish. It's beer-battered." Ivy Mae rubbed her hands together, "And their garlic bread is really yummy."

"Skipper's it is." Iris picked up her handbag and followed the other two out the front door.

Sara drove the ladies back through town and out toward the bay. Skippers sat right on the wharf with a pier extending into Blue Water Bay. It wasn't fancy, but they had access to the freshest seafood around.

"Good evening ladies. Ivy Mae, Sara, good to see you tonight."

"Francis, I'd like to introduce you to my sister Iris."

"Oh, yes, I remember Iris," Francis held out her hand. "Good seeing you. Are you here for a visit?"

"No, she's moved back here, just today," Ivy Mae beamed proudly.

"Well welcome back to Blue Water Bay. Thanks for coming here to Skippers for dinner." Francis walked them to a table in the center of the room and handed them each a menu before continuing. "Tonight, the specials include fresh rock cod, scampi prawns, and sea scallops." A man at a neighboring table waved at Francis, she nodded in return. "You ladies take your time, look the menu's over and I'll be right back to take your order."

Francis picked up a pitcher of tea and made her way to the neighboring table.

"This place appears to do a good business." Iris glanced around at the full tables.

"And for good reason." Sara set her menu aside. "They have the best seafood around. We'll come back during the day some time and sit out on the patio outside. They have a lovely view of the bay.

"Alright ladies, did I give you enough time?" Francis asked looking from person to person.

They all nodded and placed their orders. Iris and Sara ordered the pan-seared scallops with basmati rice and Ivy Mae ordered the beer-battered fried cod and fries.

"So, Aunt Iris, now that you're retired, what do you think you're going to be doing?"

"Ivy Mae told me she has been working on a garden in the back yard. She also told me about the botanical garden and its expansion. I'm wondering if they are needing volunteers?"

"You should check with Ruby."

Ivy Mae interrupted her niece, "She's such a dear. Sara's right, Ruby'll be the one to talk to. She's in charge of the volunteer program over there. She does a lot of work in the greenhouses, with seedlings and that sort of thing.

Sara continued where Ivy Mae left off. "You should have Ivy Mae show you around tomorrow."

"That's my plan," Ivy Mae said.

Iris reached for her napkin, placing it in her lap before responding. "As long as you don't make me ride a bike, I'd love to."

"Technically it's a tricycle. And I still don't see what you have against riding one."

Sara's hand came up in an attempt to cover her laugh. She loved watching the banter between her two aunts. They must have been quite the pair growing up.

Ivy Mae was not about to give up. "You really should try

my trike out. It's got three wheels for crying out loud. It's not like you're going to tip it over or anything."

"I'm not worried about tipping over. I'm concerned about how my seat will feel about a bike seat. Plus, it's been too many years since I've ridden a bike, I'm too old to start riding one now."

"Nonsense. For your information, my trike seat is wide and extra padded. It's actually quite comfortable."

Iris snorted, "I don't believe it."

"Well, you'll never know, until you try it," Ivy Mae responded. "So, I don't want to hear another word about the seat being uncomfortable until you give it a try."

"Here we go ladies," Francis arrived back at the table with the seared scallops. She looked over at Ivy Mae, "I'll be right back with your plate in a sec." Before she could walk away her husband, Dennis came bustling out of the kitchen with the other plate.

"Here you go Ivy Mae," he set the plate down. "I had to come out to say hello to Iris. It's been way too long."

"Hi, Dennis. Glad to see you and Francis are still cooking up some great seafood here."

"Thanks. I gotta get back to the kitchen. You ladies eat up." He turned and hurried back through the swinging double door.

"Enjoy ladies. Let me know if I can get you anything." With that Francis left them to enjoy their dinner.

Iris speared into a piece of scallop, "Oh my goodness, I haven't had seafood this good since I don't know when. These scallops practically melt in your mouth. Ivy Mae, you want to try one of mine?

"Be happy to, can you deep fry it for me?" Ivy Mae's eyes crinkled at the corners as she laughed.

"I've missed this," Sara smiled.

"Missed what?" Ivy Mae plopped a generous amount of ketchup onto her plate.

"You two together. The way you act with each other. Sometimes it's hard to believe you're identical twins. You two can be so different from each other."

"Us?" Iris asked looking at her twin. "Different? Good heavens no."

"We're not different." Ivy Mae finished her sister's thought. "What a silly thing to say. Two peas in a pod, we are."

Sara grinned to herself, "No, of course not. My mistake, what was I thinking?" she mumbled. "Listen, Aunt Iris, since you're going to be out and about tomorrow, why don't you stop by and I can show you what I've done with my B&B."

"I'd love to see it. It's been what six years since I've been in our old childhood home?"

"Seven, sister, not that I didn't like going to the city to see you. But I'm more of a small-town sort of gal."

"I'm with you auntie. I enjoy myself so much more here. It just feels so much more homey."

"It is going to be an adjustment for me, but I'm sure I'll get used to it. I'm happy to be close to you both. There's nothing like family. You both are so very important to me."

Ivy Mae dug a tissue from her pocket and dabbed at her eyes. "Don't make me cry, sister."

"Before you make me cry too, what do you ladies say to a little dessert after we finish?" Sara asked.

"I'm in," Ivy Mae piped up. "Their cobbler is wonderful. So is their banana pudding."

"Don't forget the chocolate cake."

The ladies relished their dinners almost as much as

their time together that evening. A little while later, Sara handed her now empty plate to Francis.

"Did I hear you ladies talking about dessert?" Francis circled the table collecting all the dishes. "Tonight, we have our famous double chocolate cake, banana pudding, and blackberry cobbler. What can I get for you?"

"Cobbler," both Iris and Ivy Mae said at the same time.

"I'll take the chocolate cake," Sara piped up "and with some coffee too. Thanks."

"Ladies, can I get you some coffee too?"

Iris and Ivy Mae looked at each other, "Decaf for both of us," Iris answered while Ivy Mae nodded.

"Be back in a sec."

While they waited for our dessert, they noticed a young woman entering the restaurant. Sara raised a hand to wave her over.

"Aunt Iris, let me introduce you to my friend Cora. Cora this is my Aunt Iris. She just moved to town today."

"Cora, how nice to meet you."

"Welcome to Blue Water Bay." She frowned and cocked her head to the side. "Was that you in that car accident this morning?"

"Yes, unfortunately, it was."

"I hope you're alright. That crash was really loud, that's for sure."

"Oh, I'm not doing too badly." Iris chuckled, "We'll see how I'm doing tomorrow. I would imagine I'll be a bit sore. I saw your ah... group in front of City Hall."

Ivy Mae spoke up, "Yes, that was them. She's going to stop them from putting those dreadful condos in. I can't imagine what they must be thinking, wanting to put them there anyway. It's hardly accessible and it would be awful for the wildlife refuge and botanical garden for that matter."

"We'll see. We're doing our best, but somedays it doesn't seem like it's going to be enough."

"Here we go ladies, chocolate cake and cobbler," Francis set down the desserts. "Hey there Cora. Good seeing you sweetie. Ladies, I'll be right back with your coffee. Cora take a seat anywhere and I'll be right with you."

"Goodbye ladies. I won't keep you anymore. Iris, it was good meeting you. Enjoy your dessert and maybe we can talk again later."

"Goodbye Cora," Sara shook her head as her friend walked away.

"What's that look for?" Ivy Mae asked.

"I don't know, I can't help but feel like she's fighting a losing battle. You know going up a big corporation. It's an uphill battle that's for sure."

Ivy Mae looked up from her cobbler, "Well you know what they say, anything worth having is worth doing well."

Iris frowned at her sister, "What? Don't you mean anything worth having is worth fighting for?"

Ivy Mae held a forkful of cobbler halfway to her mouth, "Yes, that's what I said."

Sara sat quietly eating her cake, knowing she wasn't about to get in between those two.

CHAPTER FOUR

IVY MAE WALKED to the bottom of the staircase and called out, "Breakfast is ready, sister."

Iris's head popped out of the bedroom. "I'll be right down."

The toast popped up in the toaster and Ivy Mae grabbed the plate of scrambled eggs and toast before walking out to the table in the sunroom. Ivy Mae called it a sunroom, but it was actually a large glassed-in porch that ran along the back of the house. Windows circled three sides of the rectangular room, which gave a view of her entire backyard. The morning sun warmed the comfortable space, making it Ivy Mae's favorite room in the house.

Iris joined Ivy Mae at the little table in the sunroom. "Oh, you've painted out here."

The walls were now painted a pale ice blue. "What do you think?

"I love it. It goes well with your white wicker furniture. I don't think I've seen your new cushions either."

There was a table at one end of the long narrow room with a sitting area in the middle of the room. Iris noted the pair of binoculars left on the little table by the wicker settee. An easel and a small shelf of paints and brushes stood in the far corner.

"No, I suppose not. I enjoy sitting out here, watching the birds, working on my painting."

Iris looked at the easel, "I haven't painted in so long."

"That's easily remedied. Now that you're here and have more time, maybe you can start painting again."

"Maybe. This breakfast looks wonderful. Thank you and I'm sorry I wasn't down here earlier. I sure don't expect you to cook breakfast for me every morning. I guess I was just a little slow moving this morning."

"No worries sister. I'm so happy to have you here. After yesterday, I wanted you to be able to sleep in a bit. How are you feeling this morning?"

"A little stiff, but overall, I'm fine."

Ivy Mae spooned a hefty dollop of orange marmalade on her toast. "What would you like to do today?"

"I thought it would be fun to check out the botanical garden and maybe walk through the town. I'll bet the shopping district has changed quite a bit since I was last here. I saw a little bit of Main Street before my accident."

"Sounds like a good plan to me. But before we go, I have a surprise for you."

"Ah, that's so thoughtful of you, but you sure didn't have to get me anything."

"Let's finish our breakfast and I'll show you what it is. You're going to love it." Ivy Mae's eyes sparkled with mischief behind her red frame glasses.

A while later, after their breakfast dishes were loaded in the dishwasher, Ivy Mae turned to her sister. "Okay, are you ready?"

"I sure am, just let me get my purse and I'll be right back." Iris turned to head toward the staircase.

"No, wait. What about your surprise?"

"Oh, I didn't know that's what you meant. Yes, I'm ready."

Ivy Mae grabbed her sister's arm, "Then come this way." They walked back to the sunroom and Ivy Mae stopped her sister right in front of the back door. "Alright, now close your eyes and wait right here."

"Ivy Mae, what are we doing? Why do I need to close my eyes?"

"Because I said so," her sister snapped back cheerfully.

Iris smiled, "As I recall that has always been one of your favorite responses."

"Well, sometimes it's the only response that would work with you. You always were the bossy twin. Now stand here and close your eyes."

Iris shook her head but did as she was told. "I feel ridiculous standing here," she mumbled.

"I heard that." Ivy Mae opened the back door. "I don't trust you, cover your eyes."

Iris huffed but did as she was told. Ivy Mae eased out the door and tiptoed down the pavers in the backyard. A few minutes later, Iris heard her again, "No peeking." A few seconds later when she thought she had everything ready, she yelled, "Surprise!"

Iris moved her hands and opened her eyes. There in front of her was a three-wheel baby blue tricycle with a big white bow. A blue helmet sat crookedly on Ivy Mae's head, her arms up in the air and a huge smile on her face.

Iris's mouth fell open. She wasn't sure what she expected but this certainly wasn't it.

The smile faded from Ivy Mae's face when she saw the concern on her sister's face. "You don't like it?"

"No, I wouldn't say that," Iris mumbled. She surely didn't want to upset her sister, even if it was a tricycle. "It's just like I told you yesterday. I haven't ridden anything like this ever and it's been years since I've even been on a bicycle."

"This should be a piece of cake, remember, three wheels. And look I had them add this cute little basket too. Here's your helmet. Come try it out and I'll go get mine."

Iris took the helmet from her sister and hugged her. "Thank you. This was so...ah thoughtful of you." This definitely would not have been the surprise she would have picked out for herself. And she still had a fair amount of skepticism about it, but like it or not, she was going to have to give it a shot.

Ping ping. Iris looked over to see her sister sitting on her own tricycle with her red helmet securely fastened.

Ivy Mae laughed, "Come on sister. Just give it a try."

Iris looked at the helmet she now held in her hand and then at the shiny blue tricycle. *Well, what would be the worst thing that could happen? It did have three wheels after all.* There was no time like the present. She snapped on the helmet, adjusting the strap, and climbed on. "Here goes."

"Follow me, sister." Ivy Mae pulled out pedaling leisurely down the street.

"Oh, my goodness. I can't believe I'm doing this." Iris called out.

"I knew you'd like it!" Ivy Mae turned carefully onto the road to the botanical garden. In less than ten minutes, they pulled into the parking lot for the botanical garden. Ivy Mae hopped off her bike, removed her helmet, and fluffed her silver pixie cut. "So, what did you think?"

"Well, it wasn't as bad as I thought it would be."

"See, I told you."

"If I could just get this helmet unsnapped."

"Here, I can help."

"No, I think I got it." Iris lifted the helmet off and ran her fingers through her bob. "What must my hair look like."

"It looks as good as always. Clip your helmet over the handlebars and let's get going. You're going to love the gardens."

A few minutes later they were winding their way through the Heath and Heather Collection.

"You're right Ivy Mae, they have really expanded. It's beautiful. I think I might need a map to find my way around now."

"You'll get used to it. Come on next up is the perennial garden. The raised beds were interspersed with shrubs and trees."

"Look at all these colors. I'm not even sure what all these flowers are, but the beds are so pretty."

"They should be labeled, but it looks like some of them are missing. I think these are blazing stars, these pink ones are zinnias, and those of course are coneflowers. I love watching the butterflies flitting through here. They have many different collections as they call them."

"What do you mean?"

"They have a Magnolia section, and both a camellia and fuchsia collection just to name a couple. The Magnolia's and the Camellias have quit blooming. You should see it, they have a magnolia tree with pink blossoms. I've thought one of those would look so pretty in the yard. I wish I had one." The sisters came to a fork in the path. "Over that way is the fuchsias," Ivy Mae pointed at them. Give them about another month and come back to check them out. They are gorgeous. I hear they really attract hummingbirds."

The gravel path wound around another corner and a gasp escaped from Iris, "This is beautiful."

"They call this the rhododendron trail." The sisters strolled under an archway of flowers. They have more than a thousand different rhododendrons here. Isn't it beautiful?"

Iris looked at her sister, "Do you have any of these in the yard?"

"Yes, two dwarf ones. They're purple and are going to be so pretty when they bloom."

"What do you think you're doing?"

Iris and Ivy Mae heard an angry voice coming from around the corner.

"Nothing, I was just pouring out my drink."

"What kind of fool are you pouring a can soda on the roses here. You trying to kill 'em? What'd you think those garbage cans are for? Go on take that can and get out of here."

Iris rounded the corner in time to see a young man walking away. If she recalled right, this was the same man she had seen the day before. The one Cora was screaming at about the condos.

She wasn't sure who the other man was, only that from the look of his shirt he worked at the botanical garden.

"Hey, wait a minute, you're that guy! Justin Cox!" The gardener's lip curled as he spat out the man's name.

Justin turned back to look at the gardener.

"You've got some nerve being here. Get outta here."

Justin took one final look at the man and stalked off, throwing the aluminum can in the trash.

Iris watched as the gardener began tending the roses. A

woman wearing a straw work hat and work apron walked up.

"Norman is everything okay? What's going on?"

"That doofus was pouring his can of coke out here on the roses."

"He probably didn't know better. And no more than he poured out probably won't hurt them," the woman said, trying to soothe Norman's ruffled feathers.

"Might not, but look at 'em. These over here were already lookin' bad. I can't figure out what's wrong."

"Well Norman, if anyone can figure it out, I know you can. Is there anything I can help you with?"

"No Ruby, I got this."

CHAPTER FIVE

IVY MAE ROUNDED the corner and caught up with her sister. "This area back here is new. They put in a rose garden not too long ago. Most of the roses here are the original rose varieties that were brought here by settlers back in the nineteenth century or ones that were found in the wild. There are also hybridized roses from the mid-1800s to the early 1900s." There were multiple rose beds. Some with roses blossoming in shades of white, yellow, pink, and peach.

"Aren't they beautiful?" Ivy Mae lead the way down the gravel path, bees buzzed and the faint smell of lemons filled the air.

"These are so pretty." Iris cupped a rose blossom with frilly pale-yellow petals.

Ivy Mae bent down and adjusted her glasses to read the faded marker. "It says this is the Yellow Lady rose."

"It sure does smell good doesn't it?" Ivy Mae and Iris both turned to see the woman now standing behind them.

"Ruby!" Ivy Mae reached out to hug her. "Good to see you.

"Good to see you too, Ivy Mae. Let me guess, this must be your sister?"

Iris stepped closer and held her hand out. "I'm Iris. Happy to meet you."

"Glad to finally get to meet you too. Ivy Mae has told me a lot about you. So how are you feeling about life in our quiet town."

"It was time. I'm glad to back here and closer to Ivy Mae."

Ruby glanced at her watch, "By any chance are you ladies about ready for a break? I was just headed to the cafe for some lunch."

The sisters looked at each other. "I think that would be lovely," Ivy Mae answered.

"Give me about five minutes and I'll meet you by the front gates." With that Ruby took off, the gravel crunching in her wake.

Iris looked over at her sister, "She seems nice."

"She is a really sweet lady. Unfortunately, her husband cheated on her with some young floozy about four years ago. She's still trying to get over it. It really did a number on her self-esteem."

"Poor thing, that must have been awful. Does he still live around here?"

"No, thank goodness. He moved away a couple of years ago. I think it's gotten easier for her now that he's gone."

"Come on, we should probably head on out. We don't want to keep her waiting."

"I'm coming, ladies! Sorry I got hung up back there," Ruby's purse bounced on her hip as she hurried toward the ladies.

"We're fine, no need to rush on our accounts," Ivy Mae reassured her.

"I'm looking forward to lunch at the diner. It will be my first time back there in years."

"You're going to love it, sister. They have such a good fried chicken sandwich."

"You and your fried food. Ivy Mae, do you ever eat anything healthy?"

"Iris, who says that chicken sandwich isn't healthy? It has an apple and pepper pesto."

"Don't worry, Iris, the diner has quite the variety on their menu. Healthy options and items traditionally considered as comfort food."

The smell of the salty sea blew on the warm breeze. Iris inhaled deeply, "I've definitely missed that fragrance.

They continued down the road and passed multiple shops. Colorful canopies fluttered over the front doors and windows, while large flower pots ovweflowed with blossoms. Ruby reached out to open the door to the cafe. "Here we go."

A blue, green, and white striped canopy covered the large front window. The diner was a family-owned establishment. Brenda worked as the main waitress while her grown son, Hank was responsible for the kitchen. Booths lined the right wall with a view out onto a sidewalk. The rest of the room was occupied with Formica topped tables and wooden chairs with blue vinyl cushions. Swivel seat lined the short counter in front of the pass-through window.

"How about the booth over here by the window?" Ivy Mae lead the way and passed out the menus when they were settled.

"It smells so good in here." Iris opened her menu and began to browse.

Ruby laughed, "I think that's the meatloaf you're smelling. It's one of their specials. My only problem is deciding which sides I want to go with it." Ruby studied her menu a few minutes more before setting it aside.

"I know what you mean. Iris do you know what you're going to get?"

"With the way that meatloaf smells, I think I'm going to try it."

"Hey, ladies, good to see you."

Ivy Mae glanced up from her menu. "Brenda, you remember my sister Iris."

"Well, look at you. It's been too long. I heard you moved back."

Iris frowned, "You heard?"

"The sheriff was in here yesterday, he filled me in. Anyway, our special today is meatloaf. I can give you a minute if you still need to look at the menu."

Iris looked up, "No, I think we're ready."

They placed their orders and it wasn't long before they were rewarded with plates full of yummy goodness. Meatloaf, fluffy mash potatoes with a puddle of butter and veggies. Ivy Mae and Iris had both chosen the confetti cream corn as their other side, while Ruby had selected green beans. Brenda made one more trip to their booth, setting down a basket full of the cafe's famous fresh-baked rolls.

"Oh, I thought last night's food was good, but this is amazing."

Brenda had been pouring tea at the next table, she stepped back to their table and put her finger to her lips. "Shh, don't tell Dennis and Francis that."

Ivy Mae twisted her fingers in front of her lips, "Not a peep."

"I'm teasing, they have amazing seafood and Dennis is

an incredible cook. Enjoy your lunch ladies. I'll come back and check on you in a bit."

"So, what have you ladies been up to?" Ruby asked in between bites.

"Ivy Mae was showing me around the garden this morning."

"Did she tell you about the proposed condos?"

"Seems like I hear about the condos everywhere I go."

"That doesn't surprise me, it's a really hot topic in town right now. It's got everyone stirred up. Do you know where you were in the rose garden this morning? Well, if you continue on that path and exit the garden, then take the trail to the right it will eventually bring you to the tract of land in question."

Ivy Mae picked up the story, "Yes, it's a wedge-shaped piece of property that overlooks the ocean. I can see why it's a popular site. There has been talk about the botanical garden buying it. Or the city buying it and putting in a city garden. But as with most things involving the city, it just takes time."

"And money," Ruby piped up. "Once I heard it might require a vote. And as you can imaging in the meantime, someone else has moved in to purchase the property."

Iris had been listening closely to the other two ladies. "And the young lady we met last night, what is her story?"

"Cora? She is an environmental and animal activist. She believes that building a condominium complex there, even a small one will affect the many species of birds that nest in the animal preserve. There are a couple of endangered species that stop there on their migratory path."

"I saw her on my way into town. She was having what looked like a particularly heated exchange with a gentleman."

Ruby's head popped up, "Was it a young guy? Sharp dresser?"

"Now I didn't get a very good look, but I'd say so."

"That was probably him."

Iris's head swiveled back and forth between the other two women. "Who's him?"

Ivy Mae picked up her tea and looked at her sister, "Justin Cox."

"I take it he's the one who wants to buy the land for the condos?"

"Ha! He'd be the one alright," Ruby snorted. "He can sure stir things up around here. The town is split in two over this."

"Really?"

Ruby continued, "Split right down the middle. You have those who support the animal rights community and then you have those who look at what the condos could do financially for the town."

Ivy Mae picked up where Ruby left off. "More folks in town to eat at the restaurants, shop in the stores here."

Iris sat quietly, staring out the front window for a few moments before returning her attention to the other ladies. "Hmm, I suppose I hadn't given it that much thought. And for a town this size, extra income can be very important."

"I suppose, but it would ruin the ambiance of the garden and the wildlife refuge. Just imagine, the peace and quiet would be gone," Ivy Mae protested.

"Well, what we do know ladies is, that it's not up to us," a heavy sigh escaped from Ruby. "We can only hope for the best."

"How are you ladies doing over here?"

We all nodded and Brenda continued on her way.

Iris took her last bite. "I don't know about you ladies, but this meatloaf is amazing."

Ivy Mae threw her head back, merry laughter ringing out. "I knew you would like it here."

Iris grinned at her sister, "I think moderation is the word for both of us."

"I can agree with that."

"Come to the city council meeting, come to the city council meeting." A young woman moved from table to table handing out bright yellow flyers. The woman walked up to their table and handed Ivy Mae, Iris and Ruby each a flyer, reminding them to come to the meeting. Brenda met her as she approached the next table, "Why don't we just put one of these flyers on the bulletin board. Here give me two more and I'll tape them on the inside and outside of the front door."

"Thanks, the young woman responded."

"Now how about you let everyone else eat in peace."

"Sure, no problem, sorry about that Brenda."

"No worries, dear," Brenda held up the flyers as the woman turned to walk away. "And I'll be there." Brenda walked over, grabbed a couple of push pins securing one flyer up on the corkboard by the cash register. "Sorry about that folks."

Ruby looked over at her other two lunch companions, "Will you two ladies be there?"

"Of, course we will," Ivy Mae answered firmly.

"We will?" Iris asked.

"Most definitely. I love walking through the wildlife refuge, watching the birds. It's so peaceful and quiet over there. I would hate for them to have to build anything back there. Plus, I can take the trail from there down along the coast to the botanical garden."

Iris thought for a moment before continuing, "Do you think the town could benefit from having the condos built?"

"Oh, I can see what some might perceive as a financial benefit, but I also think there's more to life than money. If we can help preserve some of the species of birds that come through here, well I consider that priceless."

Iris looked over at Ruby, "Sounds like we'll both be there."

"Well ladies, it looks like my meatloaf was a hit," Brenda laughed as she picked up the now empty plates. "Can I get you any dessert today?"

Ruby dug some cash out of her purse. "None for me, I'm going to have to get back to work. "Ladies this was fun..."

Her voice was cut off by the rise of voices right outside of the cafe.

CHAPTER SIX

ALL FOUR WOMEN turned to look out the window. Two men stood almost toe to toe. One man was dressed in jeans and a T-shirt with AA Plumbing stitched onto the pocket. A vein throbbed at his temple and spit flew from his mouth.

"Oh my goodness, Frank what are you doing?" Ruby sat at the table watching the man on the other side of the window.

Iris looked over, "Who's Frank?

Ruby never took her eyes off the two men. "Frank owns a plumbing company here in the area. He can be a little..."

"I think the word is quick-tempered," Brenda interjected herself into the conversation.

"Why are you double-parked here? You're blocking my van? You think just because you drive a fancy car that you can park it wherever you like. I'm trying to get to a job, but you've got me boxed in. You better be glad I didn't have you towed."

"Listen, buddy, there wasn't anywhere else to park. I knew I'd only be a minute."

"Well, your minute was up fifteen minutes ago. I

know what you're doing. You're running around town trying to convince folks that those condos are a good thing. You don't fool me. And let me tell you," Frank poked a finger at the other man's chest, "Your money doesn't mean anything to me. You have no business here. Why don't you get back in your fancy car and go hound someone else?"

"Listen, I don't even know who you are. I don't have a problem with you. I'm just trying to complete my business."

"You might not think you have a problem with me, but you do. Just get into your fancy car and take your business elsewhere."

Ivy Mae leaned over and whispered to her sister, "And that's Mr. Cox. I think his first name is Justin. And yes, he's the one who wants to build those condos. The smaller, nicely dressed young man turned and stalked over to his car with a frown on his face.

"Well, you don't see that every day," Brenda commented, still ogling the scene outside the window. The other ladies had forgotten she was even still standing there.

"Brenda, I think it's over." Ruby patted the lady on the arm.

The color rose on Brenda's cheeks. She swiped her hands across her apron, "Guess I'm just a little nosy, aren't I?"

Ivy Mae leaned over and whispered, "We won't tell anyone."

"That's the man I saw this morning," Iris said. "In the botanical garden. He poured a soda out on some of the roses. One of the gardeners was taking his head off for it."

"You saw that, did ya?" Ruby shook her head. "That would have been Norman. He's very protective of those roses. They're his babies."

"Looks like Justin isn't so popular in Blue Water Bay," Iris said.

Ruby said her goodbyes and slide out of the booth, headed back to work. Ivy Mae and Iris lingered for a bit over their tea before leaving.

The sisters took their time as they strolled down the sidewalk browsing in the shop windows, following their lunch. Various large clay pots dotted the sidewalk. Some were packed with dahlias and creeping comfrey, others planted with bee balm and coneflowers. Decorative street lamps were lined up and down the sidewalks. Some shops even sported window boxes overflowing with flowers of various colors. It was the image of a perfect picturesque downtown.

"I must say, the downtown area has added so many cute little specialty shops since I was here last. They've really spruced up the place up. I can see why you get tourists here." Iris looked over at her sister and laughed, "How often do you go shopping in this little fudge shop?"

"You'll be happy to know, that it's pretty rare that I actually purchase anything in there.

About that time, the little bell over the door tinkled as door of the fudge shop opened. The edges of the shop's red and white canopy flapped merrily in the breeze. The name painted on the window in big red letters proclaimed the store, The Fudgery. "Hey, Ivy Mae. Good to see ya'." A woman with a blond pixie cut, a red and white striped apron, and red frame glasses set up an A-frame chalkboard sign outside the shop. "Maybe we can plan on you coming in one day, say in the next couple of weeks to help me out. Think you can do that?"

"Sure, I'd be happy to. Iris, this is Patti. She owns The Fudgery."

"Nice to meet you Patti," Iris said shaking the young woman's hand.

"Ivy Mae, I'll bet you're glad she's here now?" Patti looked over at Iris, "She's been talking about you moving here for weeks now. Welcome to Blue Water Bay."

"Thank you, Patti." Iris glanced back and forth between the two ladies, "Do you work here Ivy Mae?"

"Oh, I just come in every now and then to help out a bit."

"She's amazing. She comes in to help me out occasionally, especially as the tourist season picks up. But don't worry, I make sure not to overwork her. I love having her around, she's so good with the customers. Listen, I won't hold you ladies up, enjoy your day." Patti waved as they turned to move on down the sidewalk.

Iris laughed, looking over her sister, "And that's why you don't have to buy the fudge, she probably gives it to you."

"Maybe," Ivy Mae admitted with a sly little smile on her face.

As they worked their way back down to the botanical garden, they passed Main Street Creamery, a local ice cream parlor.

"Oh, we've got to go in here," Ivy Mae grabbed her sister's arm and practically drug her into the ice cream shop. They make their own waffle cones."

The smell of freshly baked waffles wafted through the air as they entered. "I can tell. My mouth is watering just walking in here."

A young woman with teal-colored hair popped up from behind the counter. "Ivy Mae, hi! I haven't seen you in a while. And you must be Iris. I'm Zoey," a broad grin flashed across her face. "What can I get for you today?"

Ivy Mae had been browsing through the ice cream flavors, "I think I'd like a double scoop. One caramel nut and the other chocolate brownie chunk."

"Plain waffle cone or chocolate-dipped?"

Ivy Mae laughed, "You never have to ask me that. I'll always take a dipped one. Thanks, Zoey. Iris, what are you going to get?"

"Well, I think I'm going to splurge and get the blueberry pie."

"Good choice," Zoey said. "We get the blueberries locally. Double scoop?"

"Ah, no, just a single scoop, especially after the lunch I had."

Zoey dug into the ice cream, smashing it down deep into the cones, then piling it high. She handed the first one to Ivy Mae, then scooped what seemed to be an extra generous amount into the cone she handed to Iris. "Welcomed to town Iris."

"Thank you, Zoey. It's a pleasure to meet you. I don't think your shop was here, last time I was in town."

"I've only been open about a year now. Which reminds me ladies I'll be planning a one-year anniversary special to celebrate. It won't be for about another month."

"Wonderful," Ivy Mae took another lick of her chocolaty treat. "We'll look forward to it."

"The blueberries in the blueberry pie bits are wonderful."

"They are, aren't they. I'm glad you like it. They are locally sourced. I'm really fortunate that they grow so close. I think fresh ingredients make my ice cream taste so much better."

"I agree. This might be the best ice cream I've ever had. It's so creamy."

Ivy Mae started to fish some cash out of her pocket.

"No, today's ice cream is on the house."

"We can't let you do that," Iris protested.

Zoey held up her hands. "Happy to do it. Iris, you can consider it my welcome home treat to you."

"Thank you, Zoey. That's so thoughtful of you. Trust me you've made a new customer today."

"I knew you'd like it," Ivy Mae grinned at her sister and winked at Zoey.

About that time the door swung open and Charlie came in carrying a flat of strawberries. "Here's your strawberries Zoey.

"Thanks, Charlie. Stick them in the back. Appreciate that." Zoey called out to him as he disappeared around the corner into the kitchen. The little bell tinkled when the front door swung open again.

"Hey, Cora," Zoey greeted her. "What can I get for you?"

"I'll take a scoop of the strawberry cheesecake, please." Cora turned, "Hi ladies, good seeing you again. Will I see you tonight at the town council meeting?"

"You bet we'll be there," Ivy Mae answered enthusiastically. "We wouldn't miss it."

"Good. We're going to need all the support we can get. I don't know what we're going to do if we lose this fight. Things will change here in Blue Water Bay, and I'm afraid, not for the better."

"Don't worry Cora. I mean you're doing everything you can." Zoey tried to encourage her friend.

"I just hope it's enough," Cora gave a frustrated sigh, her lips set in a grim line, her voice rose. "I wish Mr. Cox had never come here. I know it's childish, but I wish he'd just pack up and go away."

Cora was so absorbed in this cause. It was going to be a shame if she lost her battle Iris thought to herself.

Charlie rounded the corner from the back room. "Hi Cora. Do you need any help before tonight?" Charlie asked rather shyly.

"I have a few more flyers that I wanted to put out." Cora patted a messenger bag that hung across her slight frame.

"I'll be happy to do that for you." He reached over hesitantly and took the flyers she offered.

"A couple each in all the shops between the beauty salon down to the fudge shop. Maybe they'll let you put them up on the doors."

"I'll do it right now." He flashed a grin and backed out the door, almost running into an elderly gentleman who just happened to be passing by.

Cora gave him a hesitant little wave as he headed out, before turning back to Zoey to take her ice cream. "What?" She asked when she noticed three pairs of eyes staring at her.

Zoey looked down at the floor and shook her head before answering. "Can't you see it? He has a thing for you."

Cora frowned, her mouth fell open and she swung around to look at the now empty door all at once. Her face flushed, almost hiding the freckles sprinkled across her nose and cheeks. "What? Who, Charlie? No, besides he hardly ever even talks to me. In fact, he mostly seems to ignore me. Today was the first time we've had any sort of conversation at all." Cora looked around at all three ladies.

Zoey shrugged, "Don't believe me, but I'll bet you I'm right."

"Well, that's no matter to me, I've got other things on my mind these days." Cora plunked money down on the counter and with that she turned and hurried out, clearly flustered.

Ivy Mae laughed, "Oh to be that young and clueless again."

"Personally, I'm happy not to be that clueless again," Iris responded. "Nice meeting you Zoey."

The sisters exited the shop, strolling down the sidewalk, enjoying their ice cream. They finally arrived back at the botanical garden settling themselves onto a bench outside the entrance.

It had been a perfect, contented day, Ivy Mae thought to herself. *Her sister was back, they had enjoyed a peaceful walk through part of the garden, followed by a good meal and ice cream. Life didn't get much better than this.* She sighed peacefully.

Iris finished her ice cream cone, tossing her napkin in a nearby trash can. "So how do you think things will go tonight?"

The mention of tonight's meeting reminded Ivy Mae of the trouble brewing in town. "Well, I would hope the city will send Mr. Cox packing," she paused to take another lick of her cone, "but I think we both know it's not that simple." She paused a few moments lost in her thoughts. Melted trickles of chocolate started to run down her cone. This caught her attention a moment later and Ivy Mae began to lick at the little rivulets. "It's going to be a shame if they really build any building back on that property. It's so quiet and peaceful back there and in my opinion, it should stay that way."

"I guess we'll just have to wait and see." Iris looked over at her sister and laughed, "You need to hurry up and eat that thing before it melts all over the place."

Ivy Mae laughed, "Here help me out." She handed her cone to her sister.

"Oh, these are good flavors too. Zoey sure is talented, I've never had ice cream this good. You know I'll be happy to go back there any time you want." She laughed handing the now less drippy cone back to her sister.

CHAPTER SEVEN

"THERE ARE SOME SEATS OVER THERE," Sara pointed out the seats to her aunts. She had volunteered to pick up the ladies tonight. They had left home early anticipating a full room with an equally full parking lot. This city council session was scheduled to specifically discuss the proposed condominiums and was apt to be a heated event. The meeting wouldn't start for another twenty minutes, but there was only a smattering of seats left around the room. Iris looked around and saw Cora sitting on the front row with many of her strongest supporters. She also spotted Brenda from the cafe, Patty from The Fudgery, Zoey from the Main Street Creamery, George McGuire the Sheriff, Norman from the botanical garden with his nephew Charlie.

About ten minutes later, the buzz in the room increased when Justin Cox entered the room. Some folks stood up and shook his hand as he walked by and others threw nasty looks in his direction. He eventually took a seat upfront across the aisle from Cora. It was impossible to miss the occasional glare between the two of them. Besides the sheriff, there were also another couple of deputies positioned at the back of the room.

"Ivy Mae leaned over to her sister and whispered, "This ought to be quite the meeting."

"And not in a good way," Iris responded. "Guess that's why those guys are back there," she said nodding her head toward the deputies. Iris nudged her sister, "That's not very many chairs up there?" The arced desk sat up on the dais with five chairs in place.

Ivy Mae shrugged. "I suppose I never thought about it. Blue Water Bay only has about seventy-two hundred residents. So, we only have the four council members and the mayor."

About ten minutes later the side door opened and the mayor and city council members filed in solemnly. *They didn't look like they were looking forward to this meeting,* Iris thought.

The mayor motioned a young boy scout up to the front and handed him a microphone. "Please stand everyone for the Pledge of Allegiance." The boy scout led the audience in the pledge, handed the microphone back, and walked back to his parents with a big smile on his face.

The city council members took their seats, adjusting their chairs, microphones, and whatever they had brought with them. The Mayor looked out over the crowd, "Ladies and gentlemen, this is a special session of the city council. I'm sure you aware we have only one item on the agenda tonight." He paused for a moment looking out over the crowded room. "Now folks, we all know we're here tonight to discuss an especially controversial topic. I expect everyone to behave in an orderly manner. Each party has the right to be heard. So, I would appreciate you speaking only when it is your turn at the microphone. Now let's get started. He adjusted his glasses, "Ms. Cora Westbrook, you have the microphone."

The whole room watched Cora as she stepped up to the microphone. "Mr. Mayor, members of the city council, thank you for letting me speak here tonight. As you know there is a proposal to build a 140-unit condominium complex and road to access the property wedged between the Blackwood Botanical Garden and the Willow Creek Wildlife Refuge.

"The wildlife refuge is a stopover for thousands of migratory birds including pintail ducks, white-fronted geese, shovelers, and snow geese. There are also mallards, wigeon, teal, bufflehead, ruddy, and ring-necked ducks. In the spring after the ducks and geese leave for their breeding grounds, the shorebirds arrive. Sandpipers, dowitchers, avocets, black-necked stilts. As the weather warms in the summer the herons, egrets, and some ducks will remain. There are also orioles, swallows, and flycatchers. Besides the birds, the wildlife refuge is also home to deer, jackrabbits, and other creatures. What you might not know, is there are lesser-known creatures in the area as well. Although they are small, there is one particular creature that is vital to the area. I am referring to one of the breeds of fairy shrimp. They are a vital source of protein for all of the migratory fowl that come through the area. If the condos are allowed to be built, the marshy areas adjacent to the wildlife refuge would have to be filled in. This would include a section of the property that has vernal pools where these fairy shrimp live. These vital pools would be destroyed and the fairy shrimp lost. Even though they are tiny, the birds in the area would lack a vital food source. This would have a disastrous effect on the whole ecosystem, and this is why I'm petitioning the city council to deny the approval for the construction of the proposed condominium complex. Thank you for your time.

Cora picked up her notes off of the lectern and the room erupted in vigorous applause. "You tell em," someone called out.

The mayor tapped his gavel on a block a couple of times before speaking. "Thank you, Ms. Westbrook. Now we will hear from Mr. Cox." There was a buzz in the room, along with some boos as he stood up and walked to the microphone. The mayor banged a gavel, "Quiet down."

As the room quietened, Justin Cox began to speak. "Mr. Mayor, distinguished members of the city council," he turned to face the audience, "and citizens of Blue Water Bay. Thank you for allowing me to address you tonight." He looked over at Cora, and then back to the council. "You have just listened to Ms. Westbrook's impassioned speech about the perceived dangers that the proposed condos will cause. And I know some of you are concerned, but let me assure you, your concerns are unfounded. The condominiums will only take up a fraction of the proposed property, which in fact will be closer to the Blackwood Botanical Garden than the Willow Creek Wildlife Refuge. We have no intention of putting any species in danger. In fact, I believe the increased revenue brought about by this project will be very beneficial to Blue Water Bay. This extra income could be used to fund additional programs that would enhance the educational programs offered by both your botanical garden and wildlife refuge. I believe this will be the best of both worlds for the little town of Blue Water Bay. I'd like to remind you that the families that will reside in those condos will be shopping in your town, and eating at your restaurants. Think of the boost to your economy and what it could do for your businesses. Given the facts, I trust the council will vote in favor of this new project. Thank you for your time and your consideration." With that he returned to his seat, giving Cora a wink, his lips twisted into a smirk.

"Thank you, Mr. Cox. Now we will hear from anyone in the audience who would like to speak. I ask that you state your name before you start and please, keep your comments to not more than ten minutes at the most."

A well-dressed woman stood up. She had beautiful blonde hair expertly styled, but her makeup couldn't hide the crinkles at the corners of her eyes. She wore a fashionable suit and her heels clicked on the wooden floor. She reached out to adjust the microphone. "Audrey Anderson. Thank you, mayor, council members. I wanted to take this opportunity to file a formal complaint against this condominium complex. As you know I live on the little rise behind where Mr. Cox is wanting to build his new condominium complex. I have a lovely view of the ocean from my back patio, as well as the garden. From my side patio the wildlife refuge is also visible. I am concerned if that property below my house is developed then I will lose the view that I currently have. You know I use my backyard when I give my parties, including the occasional charity event for the city. It's beautifully lit and the sunsets at night are a wonderful backdrop for any event I host. What are my guests going to see now, a tacky condo complex? It will be right there in my face. If any of the units face the back, then I could have people looking directly into my backyard. I'll have no privacy at all." The longer she spoke the higher-pitched her voice became. "Some of you have come to my parties, are you going to want that view destroyed? I certainly hope not. Besides the fact that when I purchased my home, I was assured that nothing would be built on that piece of property. I am sure the council will see reason. Think of the property values. You just cannot allow such a shoddy development to be built there. Why it's unthinkable! Thank you." With that, she nodded her head, turned, and stalked back to her seat.

Several of the council members exchanged glances, clearly not impressed with her arguments.

"Anyone else?" The mayor asked.

Iris watched as a serious-looking woman in a business suit stood up and walked to the podium. Her light brown hair was pulled back in a bun at the back of her neck. Her stylish blue pants suit made Iris wonder who this woman was and what she did for a living. She wouldn't have long to wait before she got the answers.

"Bernadette Bray. Mr. Mayor, thank you for letting me address the council tonight. As most of you know I am the Administrator at the Blackwood Botanical Garden. I will say that I can understand both points of view. I can understand the value of extra income and what that might mean for our town. I can also understand the potential detrimental effects that would occur as a result of having a complex of that size built in the proximity of both the botanical gardens and the wildlife refuge." She continued, "The property line will be very close to where our new rose section. As you know we are working to grow some rare native roses from around the state. I'm afraid of what the construction might do to these delicate roses."

Bernadette's points were clear and concise as she spoke for a few more minutes before taking her seat. Iris and Ivy Mae both watched as several more townspeople spoke, some supporting the new complex and others who were vehemently against it. The crowds for the most part had been orderly and respectful when others were speaking.

Finally, the mayor banged the gavel adjourned the meeting saying he and the other city council members would discuss everything they had heard. The plan was for them to meet the next day, review the information and then vote. The mayor was scheduled to announce the decision after that.

People began to file out of the crowded room. Iris looked over at Ivy Mae, "Well I guess that's it. Now we wait."

"Yes, now we wait," Ivy Mae agreed.

Sara edged her way with her aunts to the front door. Two matching pairs of eyes peaked out over Sara's shoulders as both of the sisters heard raised voices in the parking lot. The deputies were both out in the street directing traffic and the sheriff was nowhere to be seen. Over to one side stood Justin Cox yelling at Frank, the same man he had had the altercation with earlier in the day.

"Look what you did to my car?" Justin stepped to one side and pointed to the ding in the door of the shiny sportscar. "I know you did this."

Frank bent over to examine the dent. "What the heck are you talking about man. That's not even the same paint color as my van. You're crazy."

Sheriff McGuire strode over and stepped in between the two men. He put his hands up, separating them. "Step back guys. Now one at a time, what's going on?"

"He dinged the door of my car and it was on purpose. Look at that dent," Justin Cox's voice came out in an angry whine.

"Ha. He doesn't even know what he's talking about. Look at it sheriff. The paint on his car doesn't even match my van here."

Sheriff McGuire examined the sports car running his hand over the dent. "Frank you can go," he said standing back up.

"Thank ya, sheriff," Frank mumbled and climbed in his van, making sure his door didn't come anywhere near the sports car.

"Mr. Cox, sorry, but I agree with Frank. The paint doesn't match at all." The sheriff took off his hat, scratched his head before continuing on. "Son, I have to say, you're not very popular around here. Are you sure this project is worth it? Maybe you should think about another location. Or another town that's in agreement with your project."

Justin made no comment. The red splotches on his cheeks were noticeable, even in the dark. After a brief moment, got into his car, slamming the door behind him.

CHAPTER EIGHT

IVY MAE SAT in the sunroom with her twin, enjoying an early morning cup of tea. "Would you like to go for a hike down the coastal trail this morning? We could take our binoculars and see what birds we can spot."

"Oh, I think that would be fun. Let me grab my hat and I'll be right back."

Ivy Mae hopped up from her seat, "I'll grab the binoculars."

A few minutes later the two ladies were trooping down the coastal trail, their floppy hats shading their pale skin. The trail varied between dirt and weeds in some parts to gravel in others. They walked quietly, attempting to not spook any wildlife.

"Look dear," Ivy Mae pointed out a deer grazing quietly. "We don't have too many of them around here. And look over there, those are mallards."

"I love their colors," Iris gazed at them through the binoculars. "Look to the right sister, there is a great blue heron."

Iris lowered the binoculars and looked over at Ivy Mae.

"I think I'm going to need a bird watching manual if I'm going to keep this up. All I can say is look over there."

"Oh, don't worry, I have one at the house you can have. Plus, you have me, and anyway, you'll catch on quickly."

They continued down the path, crossing a worn wooden footbridge. All of a sudden Ivy Mae came to an abrupt stop. "So, this is where the border of the wildlife refuge meets the proposed property for the condos." Ivy Mae pointed off to the side, "Willow Creek and that old wire fence show the boundary."

"Guess that's why it's named the Willow Creek Wildlife Refuge?"

"You got it," Ivy Mae said.

"If you weren't looking, you'd hardly know it was there." A few more steps brought them in sight of a grassy field. In some places the marshes were clear. "This is it? I can't believe it." Iris's voice betraying her skepticism.

"Yes, this is it. It's wedge-shaped, so the trail in the front here leads across the widest portion of the property."

"Can you imagine how much dirt they will have to bring in here to build on? And I wonder if it's prone to flooding?"

"You would hope they would have already checked into that," Ivy Mae huffed.

The sisters continued their walk down the trail. It wasn't too long before Ivy Mae stopped again. "And this is the other boundary."

"Well, that's not very big," Iris commented turning around to look at where they had just come from.

The trail turned into gravel as they stepped past the border to the botanical garden.

"You know what Iris?"

"Yes, you always loved the sound of pea gravel makes when you walk on it."

"How did you know that's what I was going to say?" Ivy Mae stopped and put her hands on her hips.

"Because I'm your twin, I know you and that's what you always say every time you walk on gravel."

"Iris."

"What, there's nothing wrong with being a little predictable..." Iris kept walking.

"Iris!"

Iris turned to see Ivy Mae staring at something off the path and out of her sight. "What is it?" She hurried over to her sister's side. There before her, half-covered by some brush was a body, face down. They could tell they were looking at a man from his build and his clothing. A few roses were scattered all around him. Iris whipped her phone out of her pocket and dialed 911.

Ivy Mae listened to the call while leaning forward, straining for a better look at the body and the surroundings. There was no weapon in sight and without disturbing the scene it was impossible to tell how the person was killed. What she did notice was the condition of the rose bushes that were nearby. They appeared to be in worse shape than the last time she saw them. Their leaves yellow, some curled, some brown and dead.

Ivy Mae turned her attention back to her sister, "Yes, I understand. Please hurry." Iris hung up and pocketed her phone.

They hadn't seen anyone on the trail, but from the look of his suit, he might have been laying there all night. Ivy Mae noticed a layer of dew on the heels of the man's shoes.

"What do you think Iris?"

"What do you mean, what do I think? I think this is one

of the worst mornings I've had in a while now and I hope we're not in any danger out here." She looked up and down the path, concern filling her face.

"I think I recognize that suit." The wail of the siren could be heard in the distance. "Hurry, sister, we don't have much time."

"What are you talking about?"

"Look around, do you see any clues?"

"What!" Iris's eyes grew large, her eyebrows shot up. "You can't be serious."

"I'm very serious. Now hurry up we don't have much time, but don't get over there too close to the body. We can't disturb the scene."

"What the heck am I looking for?" Iris stammered.

"Anything that looks like it doesn't belong. Anything out of the ordinary." The wail of the sirens grew even louder. Ivy Mae went one way down the gravel path and Iris turned the other way. They met back where the gravel path met the sidewalk in the botanical garden. "Nothing. I didn't find anything."

"Neither did I," Iris responded, her voice quivering. Ivy Mae grasped her sister's hand, trying to comfort her sister.

The sound of footsteps running on the concrete caused them to turn. They both watched as two deputies ran up, with Sheriff McGuire trailing behind. One of the men carried a roll of yellow crime scene tape. He looked over at Ivy Mae. Wordlessly she reached her arm out, pointing in the direction of the body. The deputy took a second to react, then quickly located the person in question. The two deputies looked at each other and began to cordon off the area. By that time Sheriff McGuire had arrived, his face red from exertion, sweat running down his temples.

"Ivy Mae, why am I not surprised that you're here."

"Sheriff! I don't know why you're taking that tone with me. My sister and I were just out for a morning walk down the trail." She held up her binoculars from around her neck, "You see. And before you even ask, no one passed us on the trail going that way." Ivy Mae pointed over her shoulder back the direction they had come. "We didn't see anything, unfortunately. Well, except some lovely mallards and herons. Oh, and a deer."

"Ivy Mae," the sheriff bellowed. "Focus."

Ivy Mae frowned at him. "I'm trying to tell you, but you're not listening. We didn't see anyone or anything out of the ordinary. I even walked a little farther down the trail the other way. There was no one out here."

Iris put a protective hand on her sister's arm, "She's right sheriff. We didn't see or hear anything. Besides, it looks like he's been here a while. Just look."

The ladies both stepped back out of his way and watched the three men going about their work. One deputy was taking photos, while the other finished tying off the yellow tape.

"Sheriff, she's right when she says he's been here a while."

The ladies watched as the deputies performed their job. It wasn't long before they noticed Norman and Charlie standing a ways down the sidewalk in the garden. Another man joined the group shortly. Iris presumed he was the local coroner. Another deputy came trotting up from the opposite direction than the ladies had come from. He stepped up close to the sheriff and pointed over his shoulder. Ivy Mae leaned in a bit, attempting to hear their conversation.

"I guess we'll be going now sheriff," Ivy Mae said as she grabbed Iris's hand and started to walk off down the trail.

She wondered if there was anything to see farther down the trail from where the deputy had come from.

"Not so fast ladies."

Ivy Mae and Iris turned to the sheriff. "I will need an official statement from both of you. You can either wait a few minutes or stop by the station later today. And no matter which you pick, I need you to keep this under wraps as much as you can." He lifted his hat to scratch his almost bald head, "News of this is going to spread fast enough without any help from you two."

A frown creased Iris' forehead. "I don't think I like what you are implying."

"Well then maybe you should tell your sister to mind her own business."

Iris shot a glance at her sister before turning to the sheriff, "We'll be right over there on the bench."

As they walked off, the sheriff could hear Iris asking her sister. "Whatever is he talking about?"

"Oh, he's just got his knickers in a twist because I helped him solve a previous case." Ivy Mae crossed her arm over her chest. "Hmph, he ought to be grateful. I was just trying to help him out. Honestly, I don't know what his problem is."

"What in the world?"

"What is it now," Sheriff McGuire growled as he turned back to the crime scene.

CHAPTER NINE

THEY WERE in the process of moving the body when they spotted them. The victim appeared to have landed on a bunch of rose blossoms. Some were healthy-looking, while others were withered and brown.

A slow whistle escaped from one of the deputies. "Look at all these roses. If I had to guess, I'd say he cut them."

"There's a pair of clippers too," Sheriff McGuire added.

"But why?" The other deputy asked.

With all the officials focused on the scene, Ivy Mae took the opportunity to get a closer look for herself. She glanced to her right, Charlie and Norman were now nowhere to be seen. This was her opportunity. She tiptoed over and bent down peeking between the men before hastily returning to the bench. No one but Iris was aware of her movements.

"Go ahead guys, let's get him out of here."

Together Iris and Ivy Mae watched as the covered body was wheeled down the sidewalk.

"Hello ladies, the sheriff sent me over to get a statement from you." They looked up to see a deputy flipping through his small notebook. Together the two sisters relayed their brief story again for him to take notes.

"That's it?" The deputy asked when they stopped talking.

"That's it," they both said at the same time.

"Alright, thank you, ladies. I've got your phone numbers. We'll call if we need anything else."

"Did I see a bullet hole?" Ivy Mae whispered.

The deputy was still scratching notes in his notebook. "Yes, that's what it looked like," he mumbled.

"Randall!" the sheriff bellowed again.

"Oh, sorry sir." The young deputy's face reddened as he turned and walked away.

Sheriff McGuire walked over closer to the bench where Iris and Ivy Mae waited. "Thank you, ladies. You're free to go. I'm sorry, if we weren't so busy, I'd offer to get you a ride home." He always was a little more cordial when business wasn't involved.

"No need for that. We can make it back home by ourselves. Thank you." Ivy Mae tugged on her sister's arm pulling her up from the concrete bench. Instead of turning back down the gravel path, Ivy Mae led her sister into the botanical garden.

Iris whispered when they were a good way down the now concrete path, "What are you doing? Home is in the other direction."

"Just taking a shortcut."

Iris threw a glance over her shoulder. "From what Sheriff McGuire hinted at, you like to get involved in his business. Am I right?"

Ivy Mae sputtered, waving a hand, "Oh he was just fussing."

"Uh-huh. Why don't I believe that? Have you forgotten

who you're talking to?" Iris's left eyebrow arched so high it was practically hidden in her hairline.

"I do know you sister, better than you think. We might have been separated for a while now, but deep down, I don't think you've changed. Not one bit. Yes, you might be a bit more level-headed, a tad more cautious, but I know that curiosity. Don't tell me you don't want to who that dead body was."

"Whether I want to know or not, I'm sure you're going to tell me."

"Oh, and why is that?"

A crystal-clear laugh rang out from Iris, "Because you, my sweet twin sister, can't keep a secret."

"Well, fine, you've got me there." Ivy Mae shrugged.

They took three more full steps before Iris came to a full stop, "Well?"

"Oh," Ivy Mae's mind seemed to be wandering, "It was Justin Cox. Shot. Dead."

"Yes, the dead part I had figured out for myself."

They wandered a little farther down the path before stopping again. "So, who do you think did him in?" Ivy Mae asked. "There's no shortage of suspects, that's for sure."

"I have no idea, but you're right about the suspects. From what little I've seen since I've been back in town, any number of folks here might have done him in. I mean there's Cora. Everyone in town knows what she thinks of him. And who was that guy, what's his name? They've had at least two arguments that I know of."

"Frank. Yes, he does have quite the temper. There's no question about that."

"Well come on, let's get home."

Ivy Mae gasped, "We can't do that!"

"Why ever not?"

"Well," Ivy Mae sputtered, "You didn't get to see all the garden yesterday. We need to see the rest of it."

Iris's clear laughter rang out again, "Oh, sister, I wasn't born yesterday. At least you can be honest enough to say you want to poke about."

"Alright fine, I want to poke about." With that Ivy Mae stared down the forked concrete path, attempting to decide which direction she wanted to go. After a few moments, she started off, striding down the left fork. Iris shook her head and took off after her.

"Arthur, good morning."

"Hmm," Arthur shifted his newspaper just enough to see the two ladies. His round wire frame glasses perched on the end of his ample nose.

"This is my sister Iris. She's just moved here. Iris meet Arthur."

"Arthur, it's a pleasure," Iris held out her hand, but he didn't make an effort to return her handshake. Instead, he returned to his paper.

Ivy Mae moved her sister's extended hand away from the man with a slight shake of her head.

"Enjoy your paper Arthur. We'll see you later."

"Hmm. Yes, of course," Arthur mumbled before raising his paper.

Ivy Mae hooked her arm through Iris and walked her down the sidewalk. "Don't mind him. He's not a bad sort. He's just not the talker."

"That's the understatement of the year."

"You know he's on that bench practically every morning the garden is open. Sitting there reading his paper. I wonder if he saw anything this morning?"

"Would it have mattered? You said Justin had been dead a while."

"You never know though what might be important. I'll catch him later after he finishes his paper." Ivy Mae glanced around spotting Sheriff McGuire talking to Norman, one of the gardeners, and his nephew Charlie. "Look let's take this path. You didn't see this section of the garden yesterday. This area back here is the Mediterranean section. Why don't we sit here for a bit?"

Iris settled onto the bench, attempting to shake off her morning. "Alright. It is peaceful here."

Ivy Mae put her fingers to her lips and closed her eyes. Iris then realized what her nosey sister was up to.

"Thanks, Norman. Alright, Charlie your turn. What time did you leave here yesterday?"

"Just after closing. Then I went home to clean up for the city council meeting."

"And then this morning?"

"I got here with my uncle. We ride together."

"Did you see anything weird or out of the ordinary this morning? Anything suspicious?"

"Nothing sheriff. I've mostly been with my uncle this morning. I didn't know anything was going on until the deputies came running through here."

Iris looked over at her sister. She now knew why she had suggested they have a seat. They were on a totally different path than the sheriff and also had their backs to him. He probably didn't even know they were sitting there. Dwarf Olive shrubs and Olive trees blocked most of the view from one path to the other. Ivy Mae was sneakier than Iris remembered. She kept her mouth closed. She sure didn't want the sheriff to find them sitting there.

"Alright fellas, if you think of anything else you know where to find me."

Footsteps receded into the distance and Ivy Mae

glanced over her shoulder then grabbed Iris's hand. "Come on."

"Good morning ladies."

"Eek!" Iris and Ivy Mae jumped at the sound of the voice. They spun around to find Ruby standing behind them. A mischievous grin spread across her face.

"Ruby, you startled me!"

"Yeah, I could tell. Ivy Mae, what are you up to?"

"Shhh!"

Ruby glanced past the sisters causing Ivy Mae to turn. "He's not back there."

"Who?" Ivy Mae asked.

"Sheriff McGuire. That's why you shushed me. You don't want him to know you're snooping."

"I prefer to call it natural curiosity. I take it you heard about Justin Cox? So, did you see anything out of the ordinary this morning?"

"Oh, I heard alright. That sort of thing doesn't stay quiet for long. And no, I didn't see anything. Not a thing. But if you ask me, there's no shortage of suspects. I'm sure you know that already though. You saw those folks at the meeting last night."

"By the way, some of your roses back there aren't doing so good."

"I know. So far, we can't figure it out. Norman has worked so hard on them. We've fertilized and treated and they have just continued to deteriorate. It's like they are withering up right in front of us. Frankly, we're stumped."

"Well, keep at it. If anyone can figure it out, I know you and Norman can."

"Thanks, I hope so, otherwise they'll just bulldoze that area. You know Justin Cox wanted to purchase that piece of land too since it butts up against the land for the condominiums."

Iris frowned, "But that land belongs to the botanical garden. Why would they sell it off?"

"Money. That's what I heard anyway." Ruby shrugged, "The botanical garden is forever running short on funds. I don't know if they ever seriously considered selling. But I know Justin wanted it."

CHAPTER TEN

IT WAS ALMOST time for lunch when Ivy Mae and Iris left the botanical garden. They exited the garden through the front gates and turned down Main Street headed through town.

"Oh, sister. Let's stop in here. What do you think about trying a juice or smoothie?

The green and white canopy covered the front of Smoothie Goodness. "Hey ladies." A young man looked up from behind the counter as the little bell over the door rang.

"Noah, how good to see you," Ivy Mae called out. "Meet my sister Iris. Iris this is Noah Shepherd. He makes the best juices and smoothies around."

He held his hand out over the counter. A broad smile lit up his face. "Iris, good to meet you. Are you here in town for a visit?"

Ivy Mae answered before Iris could. "No, she's moved here and I think it's wonderful."

"Pleased to meet you Noah. I love your shop."

"Thanks. I guess you could say its a dream come true. I believe in the importance of eating well. I love that I'm able to lay my hands on quite a lot of fresh produce. Would you ladies like to try something?"

Iris looked up at the menu browsing through her choices. "What do you recommend?"

"We just got a fresh batch of blueberries. You could try our famous Blueberry Bash. It's a combination of blueberries, lime, and a little Greek yogurt. It's a favorite around here with the folks who like blueberries. What do you say?"

"Sounds good to me."

"Ivy Mae, what can I get for you?"

Ivy Mae tapped her index finger on her lips, browsing the menu. "I think I'll take the Banana Almond smoothie."

Iris elbowed her sister, pointing to the menu. "Oh, Ivy Mae, I think you should try the Berry, Beet, Lime, and Chia seed smoothie."

Ivy Mae stuck out her tongue, "Beets? Gosh no, they taste like dirt. They'd just ruin a good smoothie."

Noah laughed as he watched the exchange between the two silver-haired ladies. He was happy to know Ivy Mae had her sister back here in town.

After the whizzing of the blenders stopped Noah handed over the first cup to Iris and stood back to watch her reaction.

"Why this is lovely," Iris said sipping the creamy thick concoction.

"And here you go Ivy Mae, your Banana Almond Dream. Enjoy."

Ivy Mae took her first sip, swallowed, and breathed out a satisfying sigh. "Ah Noah, your smoothies never disappoint."

"And you're my dream customer Ivy Mae. You shop often and never complain. And, you appreciate our fresh produce."

"What do we owe you today," Ivy Mae stepped up to the counter, pulling a small coin purse out of her pants pocket.

"Nothing today ladies. It's on the house as a welcome to town for Iris."

Before they could respond the little bell over the door jangled. They turned to see Patty wrestling with the wind as she tried to close the old-fashioned glass and wood door.

"Phew, that wind is starting to gust out there." She smoothed her hair and turned to see three sets of eyes on her. "Is something wrong?"

"Nothing's wrong my dear," Ivy Mae scooted to her side and began smoothing her short blond hair back in place. "There we go. Much better."

"Thanks, Ivy Mae. Noah if I can get my usual, please."

"Sure thing." Noah turned to get back to work.

Ivy Mae hooked her arm through Patty's. "I hate to be the bearer of bad news and all, but did you hear the news?"

"What news?" Noah stopped shoveling ingredients into a blender.

"It's Justin. He's dead."

"Ivy Marigold MacIntyre!"

"What?" Ivy Mae turned to her sister.

"The sheriff asked you to keep this under wraps, and not blab it to the whole town."

Patty grinned. "Your middle name is Marigold?"

"That's your take-away Patty?" Noah asked.

"Well, the news about Justin is already spreading. I heard it from one of my customers."

"Yes, my middle name is Marigold. Although momma always called me Ivy Mae. Don't ask me why, but I guess over the years it sort of stuck."

Noah knocked on the counter, "Hello! People, can we

get back to the news of the day?" Noah sputtered. "Justin's dead? What happened?"

"Well, I heard he was found on the empty property, you know the future condo site, stabbed with one of Cora's picket signs. Personally, I didn't believe the sign part. You know how folks gossip around here. They never get the facts straight." Patty turned, "No offense Ivy Mae."

"None taken. I always try to get my facts straight before I pass the information along. That's why I can tell you for certain he was not stabbed to death by one of Cora's picket signs."

"And how do you know this?" Noah asked warily.

"Because we were there. Ivy Mae found the body," Iris said matter-of-factly.

"Iris Magnolia Abernathy!" Iris was still using her married name. "Now look who's telling tales."

"Well, you know you were going to spit it out anyway," Iris said matter-of-factly.

"Wow, you found the body?" Noah asked. He held out Patty's drink for her, but she wasn't paying any attention to him.

"I sure didn't hear that!" She stood there with her mouth and eyes, both open wide. Patty recovered before the sisters could comment. "So, where was he? If he wasn't stabbed with a picket sign, what did happen to him?"

The sisters looked at each other and shrugged their shoulders in a mirror image. "What do you think Iris?"

"Well, you know me. I wouldn't be saying anything, especially since Sheriff McGuire gave you strict instruction. You know he's going to blow a gasket if he thinks you're the one who spilled the beans."

"Oh, I'm not scared of him."

"You don't need to be scared of him, but you sure don't

need to poke the bear either, especially since you and he evidently have some sort of history."

Ivy Mae huffed, "He's all bark and no bite. What's he going to do, throw me in the pokey?"

Iris's mouth fell open, "I sure hope not."

Patty finally took her drink from Noah, leaned a hip against the counter, and looked over at him. "Do you think we'll ever find out?"

"Yeah, the newspaper will be out in the morning."

Ivy Mae swatted at Noah who still stood behind the counter. "Oh, you two smarty britches..."

"He was shot," Iris blurted out. "There now Sheriff McGuire can't get mad at you, sister."

"Shot!" Patty hissed. "By who?"

"That's the big question now isn't it." Ivy Mae glanced between her audience. "There's any number of folks who wanted to do him in."

"Yes, from what I saw last night, he sure wouldn't be considered the town's favorite son that's for sure," Patty said.

Iris looked around at everyone. "We saw an awful encounter between him and Frank yesterday. They were outside the diner really going at it."

"I'd like to stay and chat, but I've got to get back to the shop. Goodbye Noah, ladies." Patty leaned closer to Ivy Mae, "Let me know if you hear anything else." She gave everyone a wave and left.

"Iris, I suppose we should go too. Noah, thank you. We'll see you later."

"Good meeting you Noah."

The ladies exited Smoothie Goodness and continued on down Main Street. "Iris, look. There's Cora."

Cora was perched on a low brick wall, in front of the

city hall. A stack of picket signs leaned forgotten against the bricks.

"She looks like she's had a bad day," Iris whispered to her sister.

"You'd think she'd be happy with Justin no longer a threat."

Charlie came walking down the sidewalk in the opposite direction. He paused as he came even with Cora.

"Hello Cora," Charlie mumbled. "You doing alright?"

"Hey, Charlie."

The sisters walked up about that time and Cora looked up at the two ladies.

"No protesting today?" Ivy Mae asked. Iris nudged her in the side.

"I don't know if you ladies heard, but something happened to Justin. He's been murdered."

"We heard," the ladies answered together.

"I didn't think it would be very polite to picket today. It seems wrong and so disrespectful." She looked down at her hands.

Ivy Mae reached out to pat her on the shoulder. "You are a much better person than he was."

Iris watched the young freckled face woman. "I wonder if this will be the end of the project?"

Charlie's forehead wrinkled, "Of course it will end it. Why wouldn't it?"

Iris and Ivy Mae looked at each other, then the other two, and shrugged.

"I wonder if he's working for a company, who may continue to pursue the project?"

The sisters heard gasps that came from both Charlie and Cora.

"I just assumed the project would be over now that Justin is, you know."

"I did too," Cora said.

Iris cocked her head to the side, "I guess we'll just have to wait and see."

"I hope the project is dead," Cora muttered. "Not that I wanted anything bad to happen to Justin, mind you." She added quickly.

"I'll see you later," Charlie said. "I'm sure Uncle Norman is wondering where I am.

"Oh Charlie, before you go. Did you happen to see anything out of the ordinary this morning in the botanical garden?"

Charlie turned to look at Ivy Mae, "No, nothing. Why?"

Iris stifled a laugh when Ivy Mae glared at her. "I was just curious."

"No, I didn't see anything. I gotta go."

"You really need to stay out of this Ivy Mae. Leave it to the sheriff. That's why we have them."

"Excuse me, ladies, I think I'm going to go to." Cora collected her signs and trudged on down the sidewalk.

Ivy Mae watched her, "You know, if it were the other way around, Justin would probably be dancing in the street."

"I don't know sister it was probably just about the money for him. Cora seems really broken up."

"Yes, she does," Ivy Mae responded. "I just wonder if it's genuine."

"Ivy Mae! How can you think that?"

"Because I've lived here longer than you have. Don't get me wrong, Cora by all appearances is a lovely sort, but people can get crazy over things they are passionate about.

And that woman is deadly serious when it comes to environmental issues."

"By any chance is she passionate about Charlie?"

Ivy Mae shook her head, "Not a bit. And I hate to say it, but she could do better. Charlie can be a bit of a loose cannon. His folks thought it would do him some good to come live here with his uncle. He got into some trouble back home."

"Hmm, sounds like Blue Water Bay has all sorts of secrets," Iris said. She took a sip of her smoothie and watched Cora drive away.

CHAPTER ELEVEN

"THAT SURE WAS AN EVENTFUL MORNING," Iris said taking off her binoculars from around her neck. "I think I'm ready for a cup of tea."

"How about a little lunch to go with your cup of tea?"

"After that smoothie, I'm not too hungry," Iris said.

"I have just the thing. Go have a seat in the sunroom and I'll be right there."

"Don't you want some help?"

"No, but let Daisy out in the backyard." The tiny mixed breed dog ran to the back door when she heard her name called.

"Do you ever take her with you when you walk the trails like we did this morning?" Iris called out from the back door.

"Yes, and she loves it. I'm trying to train her not to bark so much though. She loves barking at the ducks and geese. She does have her own harness for riding in my tricycle basket.

A few minutes later Ivy Mae brought a tray into the sunroom. Iris opened the door for Daisy as she came running back to the house. The little dog ran in, making a dash for her cushy bed. She turned three times in a circle before she settled down to gnaw on one of her many toys. The tea kettle began to whistle and Ivy Mae hurried back into the kitchen.

"I didn't think I was hungry, but this looks so good," Iris called out.

"And here's your tea. This is a ham and cheese quiche, fruit salad, and cranberry tea. I hope you like it."

"I'm sure I will."

"Oh, your honey. I'll be right back." Ivy Mae hopped up from the table and scurried off to the kitchen.

When she returned, Iris spoke up. "You know I can take care of myself. You don't need to wait on me hand and foot."

"Well enjoy it today. Tomorrow you can wait on yourself," Ivy Mae laughed.

"I still can't believe that young man is dead."

"What do you mean? You saw all those people upset with him last night."

Iris huffed setting her teacup down, "Upset is one thing. Dead is something altogether different. You know what I mean?"

"Yes, I suppose you're right." The two sisters continued to enjoy their lunch in silence until Ivy Mae spoke up again. "What do you suppose he was doing out there?"

"Who?"

"Sister, keep up. Justin Cox, of course. He left the meeting last night. Where do you think we went after the meeting? Maybe the bigger question, what was he doing in the botanical garden, especially that late at night?"

Iris pushed her plate back and picked up her teacup. "Maybe someone asked to talk to him after the meeting."

"Yes, but why would they meet out there? And what about those roses?"

"Oh sister, I think you have too much time on your hands. You need a hobby."

Ivy Mae's clear laughter rang out, "That's the exact same thing that Sheriff McGuire told me."

"He seems like a nice man, I'm sure he just wants you to stay safe."

"I can take care of myself just fine." Ivy Mae was interrupted from further protesting by the ringing of her phone. "Hello."

Iris sat there watching a little bird flitting around the backyard. It had a bright yellow patch under its beak and on top of its head. She really was going to have to pull out her sister's bird watcher's guide.

"Oh my, yes. We definitely heard about that. Yes, uh-huh." There was a pause in the conversation. "We were actually there. Tonight? Yes, that sounds lovely. Then I can tell you all about it tonight. Alright, we'll see you then." Ivy Mae hung up the phone. "Sara is coming over for dinner tonight."

"Splendid. I can help you with dinner if you like."

"No need, she's bringing dinner. But you could make dessert. I try to have something sweet for Sara since she makes dinner. Maybe one of your pound cakes. You know how much I love them."

"Gladly."

Ivy Mae and Iris finished their lunch and a second cup of tea together. Iris pushed her chair back, "I better get started on that cake."

"Here I'll show you where everything is."

"No need. I can probably find everything. I mean, have you moved anything around since I was here last?"

"No, I don't believe so."

Ivy Mae listened as Iris began gathering ingredients in the kitchen. Thoughts of the murder still occupied her thoughts. Did Justin walk to the back of the garden? It was so dark back there. Why would he be meeting anyone back there?

"Ivy Mae, why do you have sheets in the kitchen?"

"Well, that puts them closer to the back door. It was really cold last winter."

A frown creased Iris's forehead. Her sister's response made absolutely no sense to her. What was her sister talking about? Could she be going a bit bonkers? Iris poked her head back into the sunroom. "So why do you need sheets by the back door?"

"To cover my dwarf hibiscus and some of my other plants of course. I didn't want them to freeze. Plus, if I stored them down here, I wouldn't have to be running up and down the stairs."

Iris shook her head slightly. "Of course, why didn't I think of that." Before long, Iris slid the cake pan into the oven. "You know it might be easier if you and I go over to Sara's house rather than having her haul dinner over here."

"You're probably right. I think she's just used to coming over here. I've always told her I could come over to her house, but I don't think she wanted me to have to come back home by myself at night. For crying out loud, she's not even five minutes away. I think she thinks I'm an old woman. I finally gave up and just let her bring everything over here."

Iris sat quietly for a moment, "I think we should give her a call."

"Go right ahead."

Ivy Mae listened to her sister as she explained the logic of them making the short trip to Sara's house than the other way around. "Yes, I understand, but we'll be fine. And I'd love to see the B&B. Yes, perfect. We'll be there."

Iris beamed at her sister. "She said yes. We're expected at 6:30 for dinner."

"Good job sister. Sara's a sweet girl, but a bit overprotective if you ask me."

"I'm sure she means well."

"I'm sure she does, but I can take care of myself. By the way, while you were working on the cake, I dug this out for you."

Ivy Mae handed her sister a bird guide book. "Oh, thank you. This is going to come in handy." Iris began to thumb through the colorful pages.

"And you can sit right here, enjoy your afternoon and watch the birds. I filled the bird feeders while you were working on the cake too."

The sisters whiled away their afternoon, watching the birds and catching up.

Before long, it was time to leave. Ivy Mae waited downstairs for her sister with her handbag slung over her arm. Daisy sat on the floor by her side, her bright pink harness on and leash snapped in place.

"I'm so excited to see what Sara has done with the B&B." The ladies got to the front door before Iris piped up. "Oh, the cake." She hustled back to the kitchen and scooped up her cake container off the counter.

In a few minutes, they stood on Sara's doorstep ringing the bell. Daisy pranced eagerly by their side.

"Aunties come on in. Sweet little Daisy." Sara reached down to ruffle the little dog's fur.

"Look, Iris brought you one of her special pound cakes."

"You know your pound cakes are my favorite." Sara took the cake from her aunt and hugged her.

"Come on in, I've got everything ready." Sara led the ladies into the dining room. Daisy scampered into the room ahead of them and hopped onto a dog bed set up in the corner.

"Oh, Sara. It's beautiful in here. Is that mom and dad's old furniture?"

"Yes, that's their old dining room table, hutch, and sideboard."

"There's something different," Iris said scanning the room.

"I had them refinished, and put the extra leaf in the table. Didn't they turn out pretty? And they're perfect for my B&B. I put breakfast out on the sideboard and my guests can help themselves."

The old family home had five bedrooms when you counted the attic that Sara had made into a large suite. She maintained her room downstairs and the guests had the rooms on the second and third floors.

"I have two rooms booked currently. But if you want after dinner, I can give you a tour."

"That sounds wonderful. I'm glad someone is getting use out of this old house."

"Have a seat and I'll be right back with dinner."

Iris glanced around the room as she pulled out a chair. "This does bring back memories, doesn't it sister?"

"It sure does. I can remember papa sitting at the head of the table with momma at the other end. We sure had some wonderful meals together."

"And now we'll get to enjoy many more here together," Sara responded as she came in through the swinging door that led into the kitchen. She held a steaming bowl of spaghetti and meatballs. "I hope you're hungry," she grinned.

The three ladies loaded their plates with salad, garlic bread, mounds of spaghetti and started in.

"Now wasn't this easier eating here?" Ivy Mae asked.

"Yes, I'll admit it was easier. But easier isn't always my concern, especially when it comes to you two."

"Why is it, folks think I can't take care of myself?" Ivy Mae

A laugh escaped from Iris, "Maybe because you are the youngest and the one who always got in the most trouble."

"Youngest, my foot. I'm only the youngest by about ten minutes."

Sara looked back and forth between her two aunts, "I have heard so many stories from my dad. To hear him tell it, you two were quite the pair."

"Don't you believe everything your father tells you. He's prone to exaggerations. He always was quite the story-teller," Iris said.

"Maybe he can come for a visit soon. It sure would be nice to be all together again, even if it's just for a visit."

"I'll work on him and see what I can do about that," Sara said. "Oh, but tell me about your escapades this morning."

Iris and Ivy Mae recounted the events of the day including their conversations with Ruby, Noah, Cora, and Patty.

Sara cocked her head to the side, "Seems like folks either really liked him or hated him, depending on how they felt about the condos. I wonder who killed him?"

"I don't know yet, but I do have several suspects."

"Auntie, I know you're not going to get mixed up in the middle of this. Aunt Iris, talk to her."

Iris coughed, almost choking on her food. "What makes you think she listens to me?"

Sara laughed, "Because she doesn't listen to me and you're her sister."

"Oh, you two," Ivy Mae laughed. "I love to get you going."

"You don't fool me. I know you're not teasing," Iris shook her finger at her sister.

"Well let's just say, I promise I won't do anything crazy."

"Good, I'm glad to hear you say that." Iris slid her chair back from the table. "Now how about dessert." She and Sara got up to take their plates to the kitchen.

"But I'm going to keep my eyes and ears open," Ivy Mae mumbled to herself.

"I heard that," Iris called out.

CHAPTER TWELVE

THE LADIES ENJOYED their evening together, but eventually they decided to call it a night. Sara packed them up some spaghetti and meatballs to take home and they sliced her a generous portion of pound cake to keep for her and her guests.

"Do you ladies need me to see you home?"

"No, of course not. We'll be fine. It's just down the road. And besides, we have Daisy with us."

"Alright, well you both be careful. Text me when you get home."

"Yes, mother," Ivy Mae teased as they left.

Halfway home Iris looked over at her sister, "You're right. She is a little overprotective."

"I suppose even more now since 'you know who' was killed."

The ladies climbed the steps to the front door and Ivy Mae yanked a scrap of paper out from the door frame, then held the door open for her sister. She opened the note after her sister entered the house. The handwriting scrawled across the page. *Stay out of this.* That was it. That was all it said. Daisy stood in the doorway and growled toward the street before running into the house. Ivy Mae took a quick glance over her shoulder. The road appeared empty, but the street lights didn't seem to light up the road like normal. Ivy Mae felt a shiver climb up her spine, making her heart beat faster than usual. She stepped into the house, shoving the scrap of paper into her pants pocket when she heard her sister approaching. There was no need for Iris to find out about this.

"That was so much fun tonight. It sure is nice being close to family again. I put the spaghetti in the fridge and unless you need anything, I think I'll turn in."

"Good night sister. Sleep well." Ivy Mae heard Daisy scratching at the back door. "I'm just going to let Daisy out before I turn in."

Ivy Mae watched her sister climb the steps then pulled the note back out of her pocket. Daisy trotted to Ivy Mae and then back to the door, anxious to be let out into her familiar backyard. "Silly dog, you just walked home." Ivy Mae flipped on the light to the backyard before opening the door. She watched as the little dog trotted around the backyard sniffing in various spots before she turned to run back into the house. Ivy Mae locked the door and took another moment to scrutinize the note. She examined first one side, then the other. There didn't seem anything out of the ordinary about the paper, but she still got the shivers while reading it. Who could have possibly left this on her door? And why? Ivy Mae jumped when her cell phone buzzed. Sara's name was on the caller ID.

"Hello, my girl."

"You didn't text me."

"I'm sorry. We made it home fine. I'm sorry, I forgot to text you."

"No worries auntie. I just wanted to double-check on you. Are you alright? You sound a little funny."

"Oh, I'm fine. Just a little tired I guess."

"Well, thanks for coming over tonight."

"You're welcome, my dear. You know I always enjoy your company so much."

"Sleep good, auntie. I love you."

"Good night my dear. I love you too." Ivy Mae pocketed her phone. About that time Daisy started to growl again while staring off into the blackness of the backyard. Ivy Mae double-checked her doors and hurried off to bed, grateful that she wasn't alone tonight.

As much as Ivy Mae tried to sleep that night, it just didn't happen. She tossed and turned. Her mind wracked with thoughts of who would have sent her that note. Someone who didn't like her snooping into the investigation had been on her porch. Sheriff McGuire didn't want her poking about. Surely, he wouldn't leave a cryptic note tucked into her door. He'd just come right out and tell her to stay out of his business. Who knew she would be looking into the murder? Had someone overheard her talking?

In the early morning hours, when her mind had quieted down Ivy Mae was finally able to drift off to sleep. She woke to hear someone moving around in the kitchen.

"Good morning sleepyhead," Iris put her hand on her hip. "You sure did sleep late today."

"I guess I didn't sleep well." Ivy Mae stifled a yawn.

"What's wrong?"

Ivy Mae looked up, "Nothing. What would make you ask that?"

Iris crossed her arms. "Spill it."

Ivy Mae reached into her bathrobe pocket and pulled out the now creased piece of paper.

Iris frowned looking at the paper. "What is this?"

"It was stuck in the door last night."

Iris's mouth fell open, "Last night! Sister, why didn't you tell me?"

Ivy Mae shrugged, "Probably because I didn't want to hear an I told you so."

Iris held her arms out and drew her sister into a hug, "You're my sister. I would never say that to you." She released her sister, holding her at arm's length, and sighed. "Well maybe I would have, but it would only be because I would be frightened for you. Go sit down at the table. I'll bring your breakfast in."

Ivy Mae did as she was told, pulling out a chair at the table in the sunroom. Puffy white clouds floated through the bright blue sky. Everything seemed right with the world, but Ivy Mae felt anything but alright.

Iris came in a few moments later with a cup of coffee and a basket of freshly baked blueberry muffins. "Here you go, this will pick you up. Let me get my coffee and I'll be right back."

The sisters were soon settled at the table together. "I hope you don't mind me using the blueberries that were in the fridge. I remembered how much you liked my muffins."

"Of course, I don't mind. And I do love your muffins, that's for sure. Thanks for making them."

Ivy Mae got up from her seat as Daisy scratched to be let back in. "You've certainly made my morning brighter," Ivy Mae said as she sat down and reached for a second muffin. "I'm beginning to feel normal again."

"Who do you suppose left that note in the door?"

"I have no idea."

"Quite frankly this makes me mad. No one has the right

to threaten you. The nerve." Iris's coffee cup clattered against the saucer as she set it down.

"Now, now sister. It's probably just a neighborhood kid playing a prank."

"I don't know Ivy Mae. That seems a bit of a stretch for a kid. Do you think we should call the sheriff?"

Ivy Mae smeared butter in the middle of her muffin. "Oh, I don't think so. It probably didn't mean anything. Why don't we flip on the news this morning and see if there's anything new regarding Justin?

There was a small television set up in the corner of the sunroom. "My name is Audrey Anderson and I don't mind saying, I'm opposed to the proposed condominiums.

The reporter held up a microphone in front of her face. "Tell me, Ms. Anderson, why are you so opposed to the building project?"

"I believe it would have a disastrous effect on our delicate environment. Why Blue Water Bay is the home of so many species of wildlife. Just imagine how their homes in the wildlife refuge would be disturbed."

"You are aware that Justin Cox was killed. Do you think the project will continue now that he is no longer involved?"

"I don't know. As unfortunate as his death was, I personally hope the project has come to an end."

"Is that because if the project is canceled, then your view of the ocean would be saved?"

"Well..." Audrey sputtered into the microphone, "I might treasure my view, but the environment is the one that really benefits if the condos are canceled.

Ivy Mae threw her head back and laughed so hard, tears rolled down her cheeks. "Someone sure has changed her tune."

"Who knows, maybe she learned something at the town council meeting."

Ivy Mae lowered her glasses and stared at her sister, "Do you believe that?"

A slow smile spread across Iris's face, "Not really. She was pretty clear the other night of what her priorities were and why she didn't want the condos built. Honestly, I can't blame her, I wouldn't want a set of condos overlooking my backyard either."

"By any chance do you feel like a ride this morning?"

"I think it would do us both some good to get out and get some fresh air."

A short while later they were snapping on their helmets. Daisy wore her pink harness and was sitting happily in Ivy Mae's tricycle basket.

"You lead and I'll follow," Iris said.

The ladies pedaled away from the house. Ivy Mae felt the last of the lingering worries float away in the breeze. It was easy to let her mind drift as she pedaled along. What was Justin doing at the botanical garden at night? Had he walked there or driven? If he drove, where was his car? She sure couldn't ask Sheriff McGuire these questions.

Iris followed Ivy Mae as they pedaled through Blue Water Bay. She had no idea where they were going, but it really didn't matter. The sun was shining, and a light breeze blew the salty smell off the ocean. They passed the botanical garden entrance and Ivy Mae kept pedaling. Pretty soon they turned their tricycles onto a small road that snaked around several curves. Pines, spruce, and the occasional cypress tree lined both sides of the road. Iris spotted a row of vacation rental cabins tucked among the trees. If they hadn't been painted a lovely shade of turquoise, she might have missed them. The sisters took one more curve before spotting the wide blue-green ocean spread out in front of them.

Ivy Mae stopped her trike and unhooked her helmet. Daisy yapped from her seat in the basket.

"This is beautiful. What a view!"

"I thought you'd like it." Ivy Mae beamed and she lifted Daisy out of the basket.

The road dead-ended into a small parking lot. A dirt path was located on the other side of a low post and cable fence. The sisters climbed off their tricycles and crossed over onto the path.

"So, if we continued down that path..."

"We'd end up behind the botanical garden," Iris finished her sister's sentence.

"Yes, exactly. And if you take the trail to the left you'll find steps that will take you down to the beach."

Iris looked around before having a seat on the nearby bench. "I don't think they had this trail put in last time I was here. I love this." Daisy sniffed around the bench and as far as her leash would let her go. Iris inhaled deeply tipping her head back to the sun. "I'd forgotten how much I loved this area."

Ivy Mae sighed, "I never get tired of this view."

They enjoyed their morning, watching the birds and listening to the waves pound the shore below them.

"I wish I had remembered to pack something for us to drink. You want to stop in for a smoothie?"

"Sounds good to me."

"Daisy let's go girl." The little pup turned to the sound of her name and took one final jump at a butterfly before she trotted over to Ivy Mae.

The ladies peddled their trikes side by side down the road in the direction they had come.

"Ivy Mae?"

"Yes?"

Iris stopped in the middle of the road, staring over to the side. She leaned over her handlebars and squinted.

"Iris, what are you doing?"

"Look!"

Ivy Mae slowed her tricycle and circled back around. "Oh, my lordy! Is that what I think it is?"

CHAPTER THIRTEEN

IRIS CONTINUED to stare at the shrubs. "Yes, I do believe it's exactly what you think it is."

Tucked behind some shrubs was Justin Cox's bright red sports car.

Ivy Mae frowned, "Why would he go to all the trouble of parking it behind those shrubs?"

"It's obvious, sister. He didn't want anyone to see his car. I would guess that he parked here, took the back trail down to the garden."

"Why?"

"I'd say he either was meeting someone back there or he was up to something."

"Something he didn't want anyone knowing about," Ivy Mae agreed with her sister.

"I suppose we should call the sheriff. He obviously doesn't know it's back here."

Ivy Mae moved her bike to the side of the road and climbed off. Iris watched as her sister started to tiptoe toward the car.

"I don't think you need to tiptoe. No one's going to hear you."

"Smarty britches, I don't want to leave any footprints or disturb anything."

"Whatever you do, don't touch anything."

Ivy Mae turned back and scowled at her sister. "Well of course not. Why would I do that?"

"I don't know. Why are you tiptoeing over there in the first place?" Iris mumbled.

"I can hear you."

"I'm pulling my phone out," Iris said.

"No, give me a minute."

"Iris, there's some white powder back here on the ground."

"Don't touch it, you don't know what it could be."

Ivy Mae made her way back. "I didn't touch anything. The white powder is on the ground and sort of underneath the car. Maybe like something was dropped out of the trunk."

"Is it okay to call the sheriff now?"

"Yes, yes Ms. Law-abiding citizen, call him."

It didn't take long before a sheriff's car came around the last curve.

"You think he's going to yell at me?" Ivy Mae asked as the car began to slow.

"From what I've seen in the past, yes."

They watched the man squeeze out from behind the steering wheel. "Ivy Mae, what are you doing?"

"Now Sheriff," Iris spoke up, "Before you start in, we were just out riding. We weren't looking for anything. We even missed it the first time we rode by."

"That's right, and besides that, Iris was the one who spotted it."

"So where is this car?"

Both ladies pointed in the direction of the shrubs that were blocking the car. The sheriff took a few steps forward until he could see the sports car. He turned back to look at the ladies. "Did you touch anything?"

"Of course not," Ivy Mae crossed her arms. "I would never do that," she said as frown lines creased between her eyes.

Sheriff McGuire turned his attention back to the car.

"I'm not that careless," Ivy Mae whispered to her sister.

They watched as the sheriff checking the scene before approaching the car. He reached for his radio when he spotted the white powder below the trunk. Ivy Mae was torn between sticking around to see what she could see and hear versus leaving before she became the target of the sheriff's wrath. Before long another deputy showed up to collect a sample of the white powder and fingerprint the car. This was followed by a tow truck that showed up to haul the car off. Even though the sheriff and his deputy were standing on the other side of the road, the sisters could still hear bits of their conversation.

"Sheriff we got a call at the station right before I left. Norman Stillwell called in to report his handgun was stolen. I thought you ought to know."

"That doesn't sound good. Thanks, Randall, I'll check it out."

Iris and Ivy Mae's heads swiveled toward each other when they heard those words. A few minutes later the sheriff drove away, leaving the deputy to take a statement from the women. It was the same information they had recited to the sheriff. When they finished Ivy Mae knew this was her chance. Maybe she could get some answers, especially since the sheriff was no longer there. The deputy was still writing, but Ivy Mae started in anyway.

"So you have any idea what that powder was?"

"No ma'am. I have no idea what it was. And if by some miracle I did, the sheriff would have my hide if I said anything. Sorry ladies." He flipped his notebook closed, tipped his hat, and walked away.

Iris looked at her sister, "Really?"

Ivy Mae shrugged, "It was worth a shot." She loaded Daisy back up in the basket and they started off. "Still want to stop off for a smoothie?"

"Definitely."

They took their time, pedaling along at a leisurely pace until they approached the botanical garden. Ivy Mae made a hard left and whipped into the parking lot. She pedaled quickly up to a car whose door had just opened. The driver was now blocked in the car where she sat, due to Ivy Mae's applying her breaks later than she anticipated.

"Ivy Mae, are you trying to run me over?"

"Oh, sorry no." Ivy Mae moved her tricycle back out of Ruby's way. "I just wanted to speak to you. It won't take but a moment."

"Of course. What's up?"

"How are your roses doing?"

"It's hard to tell currently. Norman is doing the best he can."

"Could they have been poisoned?"

"Well, I suppose that's an option. They don't seem to have any bugs or fungus, not over-watered or under-watered. I can check with Norman. What makes you think they were poisoned?"

"Justin Cox's car was located this morning. There was some sort of white powder by the trunk of his car."

"And you think it was poison?" Ruby asked collecting her things from her car.

Ivy Mae shrugged her shoulders, "I'm suspecting it was. Justin wanted the piece of property the rose garden was on. He couldn't get it, so why not take some revenge. Poison the roses. Norman caught him pouring his soft drink out onto one of the bushes."

Iris had been listening to the conversation. Her sister had a good point.

Ruby tilted her head to the side, "You don't think Norman had anything to do with Justin's murder, do you?"

"They did get into it the other day. But I don't know. Could he do anything like that?

"I don't know. Honestly, I don't know him that well. I can let you know if I see or hear anything out of the ordinary though."

"Thanks, Ruby."

"I'll see you ladies. I'd better get in there. I have some weeds waiting for me."

Iris waited until she was alone with her sister before speaking. "Do you think Norman was the one who killed Justin?"

"He sure does look like a good suspect. I mean if you had to choose between Audrey or Norman, which one would be the most likely suspect?"

"I don't know. But I do know there is a smoothie calling my name. Let's go," Iris said as she turned her tricycle in the right direction.

They pedaled down to Smoothie Goodness, parking their tricycles in front of the shop.

"I love these bike lanes," Iris said, unsnapping her helmet.

"Me too. Main street might not have a lot of traffic, but

I'm much happier riding in a bike lane. So, what are you getting today?" Ivy Mae asked as they entered the shop, Daisy prancing in with them.

"He makes slushes too, right?"

"Yes, I do," Noah answered as the ladies entered his shop.

"I kind of feel like something icy after our ride," Iris said.

"Me too. I've had the peach lemonade slush. It's really good."

Iris nodded at her sister, "Sounds good to me." Peach and lemonade weren't two flavors Iris had ever thought of putting together, but she was willing to give it a try.

"You'll love it. We got some fresh peaches in just the other day." Noah set to work on the two drinks."

Ivy Mae reached over and squeezed her sister suddenly, which caught Iris off guard. "I'm so happy to have you here."

"And I'm happy to be here with you again too. It's so much better being here with family."

"Yes, and just think, Ivy Mae now has a partner in crime," Noah laughed as he held out the two drinks. "Here you go, ladies."

Ivy Mae reached out to take the two cups, "Oh, Noah Shepherd, you think you're so funny."

"I don't know about funny, but I know, I make amazing drinks. Tell me what you think."

"Oh, my goodness. It's delicious," Iris responded, now glad that she'd tried it.

Ivy Mae agreed. "Yes, I'd forgotten how good this one is."

About that time Ivy Mae's phone rang. She glanced at the caller ID. "Let me take this." She stepped out the door, taking a seat on the bench outside the smoothie shop. Iris paid for the drinks before joining her sister outside.

"Yes, we had sort of heard that this morning. What else did they say?" Ivy Mae paused to listen to the response. "Uh-huh, uh-huh. Yes...Thanks for the call, Ruby. Keep me updated, and thanks again." Ivy Mae slipped the phone back into her pocket.

"What did she say?" Iris asked between sips of her drink.

"Sheriff McGuire stopped by the botanical garden to talk to Norman. He said he just discovered that his handgun was missing. He told the sheriff it had been several months since he had it out last, so he really didn't know how long it had been gone."

"Wow, now that's convenient. I mean really. We've seen Norman and Justin going at it. Justin has been shot and now Norman reports his gun missing. Is that a coincidence or what?"

"Or what if you ask me," Ivy Mae said grimly.

"I wonder what Sheriff McGuire thinks?"

Ivy Mae shrugged, "No idea and he'd never tell me if I walked up to ask." She reached down to pick up Daisy after she finished lapping some water from the pet bowl outside of the shop. "Ruby didn't say Norman was arrested. I wonder if the gun that shot Justin is the same caliber as the one Norman lost?"

"I wonder where Norman was after the town council meeting. Does he have an alibi?"

"I guess that's the million-dollar question."

"And think about your other suspects. Like Cora, where was she after the meeting? Or Frank for that matter."

CHAPTER FOURTEEN

"SO, sister, I hope you're ready for tonight," Ivy Mae asked while the two enjoyed an afternoon cup of tea.

"What's tonight?" Iris asked setting down her cup of tea.

"Tonight, we are having a meeting of the Taster's Club."

"The what?"

"The Taster's Club. It's a perfectly delightful club to be a part of. You'll see."

"For goodness sake sister, tell me what it is?"

Ivy Mae grinned mischievously at her sister. "It's a group of local business owners. They get together to try out new recipes on each other. We taste test new items before they get added to the menu. We give our opinions and generally have a good time together."

"Oh, well that certainly is different. And it sounds wonderful."

"We'll meet over at the diner tonight with Brenda and her son Hank. You remember Hank, he runs the kitchen there. Zoey, Noah, and Patti will be there. Sometimes Francis and Dennis come and Sara is usually there too.

She's always on the lookout for new recipes to try at the B&B."

"So how did you get invited? You don't own a food business?"

"No, I definitely do not, but it was my idea to create this little group. They used to talk about trying out new recipes and how they appreciated honest feedback. So, I thought what better way than to have a tasting party. Blue Water Bay is a small town and each of the business owners support and encourage one another. If one fails, then they each suffer. Everyone benefits from tourism, so it only makes sense to help one another. And besides that, we have a good time spending an evening together."

"Well, that sounds quite creative and no doubt, fun. Is there anything we need to bring?"

"They don't expect me to bring anything. Sometimes I do though, especially if there's something I think one of them would really like. Like my blueberry corn muffins. Brenda added them to the menu at the diner."

"Yes, I love those muffins. We should make some soon, or maybe we can just go to the diner and get some."

"I agree," Ivy Mae grinned. "Until then, do you need to go lay down and take a nap?"

"Ha! Of course not. What do you think I am? An old lady?"

"Then how about another cup of tea and let's do some bird watching."

The ladies enjoyed the rest of their afternoon, seeing mostly mockingbirds and doves with the occasional visit from a wren.

Later that evening the ladies left home, anxious to get to the diner and enjoy an evening with their friends.

"Come on in ladies." Brenda unlocked the diner door. I

think just about everyone is here. Zoey, Noah, and Patti were seated around a long table in the center of the room.

"Hello," the group called out to the sisters, waving them over to the table.

There was another knock at the door and Sara came in behind her aunts, carrying two pie plates.

"Hello aunties," Sara said giving each woman a kiss.

"My dear, good to see you again," Iris said.

"What did you bring?" Ivy Mae asked, looking at the foil-covered dishes.

Sara turned moving the dishes out of her reach, "You'll see."

With everyone seated, Brenda took charge of the group.

"Welcome everyone. Glad you could come. Dennis and Francis won't be here tonight, but I think we'll still have enough to sample." She passed out pens and comment cards for everyone. "Who would like to go first?"

The folks glanced around the table. "I can go first," Sara said. "I have brought two different types of quiche." She peeled back the tinfoil from each. "This one is a roasted red pepper and spinach. And this other one is a caramelized onion and bacon." Sara served up slim slices of each and passed them around the table. People were quiet as they sampled first one, then the other.

"What kind of cheese is in this one?" Brenda asked poking her fork at the slice of onion and bacon?"

"Cheddar," Sara admitted. "I thought about gruyere, but I thought I'd try cheddar first."

"I think gruyere might be better." Brenda took a second bite. "Don't get me wrong it's good with cheddar, I just think the gruyere might be better."

"Anyone else? Sara asked.

"Well, I like them both," Ivy Mae answered.

"Me too. But I suppose that makes us not very helpful," Iris said taking another forkful of the roasted red pepper and spinach quiche.

Noah took a forkful of quiche, "I would just recommend chopping up these spinach leaves a little more. It would make it just a little easier to eat, that's all.

"Noted," Sara said. "What do you think about the crusts? I've worked really hard to make a good, flaky crust."

"It's great. Hank and I might need to get you to make our pie crusts for us."

"Yes, very flakey," Patti admitted. "You've got nothing to worry about with your crusts."

"I loved the flavor of these roasted red peppers," Iris said

"Yes, they are really good," Brenda agreed.

"I would hope so, they were fresh and a pain to peel. I wonder if I could use jar peppers?"

Noah gasped, "Bite your tongue! You can't use jar peppers."

Brenda laughed, "Now Noah. Have you ever tried to peel peppers?"

Noah looked from Zoey to Brenda and Sara before looking down at his plate again, "Well no."

A throaty laugh exploded from Brenda. "Now that's just like a man. Telling a woman what she can't do, when he hasn't even tried it."

"Oh, let's not man bash," Zoey said coming to Noah's rescue. "Noah and I," she said hesitantly, "just love fresh produce. But," she paused looking at Noah, "that doesn't mean that some shortcuts couldn't be taken." Zoey nodded her head at Sara, "Especially if she's happy with the outcome. Personally, I love both of these quiches. I'm with Brenda, I'd love to try this with gruyere instead. But overall, you've got two winners here."

"Anyone else?" Sara asked.

No one spoke up, so they moved on. "Alright, how about I go next? This is a recipe Hank and I have been working on. We were going to add it to our summer menu. This is our new pasta salad." Brenda spooned up the salad and passed around bowls to everyone. "So, this is a bowtie pasta, tomatoes, bacon, red onions, and then the dressing of course."

"I love the fresh basil," Noah said. "I'd order this."

Iris spoke up, "I agree. This is really good."

"We made that batch today. It would actually be better the second day. You know the flavors have a chance to mingle. Just add the avocado before you eat it."

"Is this parmesan cheese?" Sara asked.

"Yes," Brenda answered. "I've wondered how it would be with a goat cheese."

"I think either would taste good," Noah said spooning a little more pasta into his bowl.

Zoey laughed, "I think he likes it."

"I definitely like it."

"Well, I agree. Here scoop me a little more please." Ivy Mae passed down her bowl.

"Don't fill up Ivy Mae, my ice cream is still coming."

"And my new smoothie."

Noah hopped up from the table and went to retrieve two thermoses, shaking them as he returned to the table.

Ivy Mae leaned over to Iris, "I hope that doesn't have any beets in it."

"I heard that Ivy Mae," Noah responded. "Don't worry, you're going to love this."

Brenda set a tray of little glasses on the table.

"Alrighty folks, wait until you try this." Noah opened the first thermos and poured seven glasses. He passed them around the table and set back watching for reactions.

Ivy Mae sniffed at the thick white liquid. "What do you call this one?"

"This is my Vanilla Cupcake Smoothie."

"Oh, I love vanilla cupcakes," Ivy Mae said taking a sip of the drink.

"This is not the kind of cupcake I'm used to," she said after swallowing her first sip.

"But it's not bad." Iris tipped her head to the side looking at her drink.

"As long as you're not expecting a cupcake," Ivy Mae practically snorted. "You might want to rename it."

"Okay, try this one." He poured another round of drinks. This time the thick concoction was a vivid shade of green.

Ivy Mae wrinkled her nose just looking at it.

CHAPTER FIFTEEN

LAUGHTER RANG OUT FROM BRENDA, "Look at Ivy Mae's face."

"Wow, look at that," Patti piped up. "It's definitely green."

"Now come on guys, no judging just because it's green." He passed the glasses out and again waited.

Each of the women picked the small glass up but were slow to try it. Several sniffed at it.

"I smell pineapple," Zoey said.

"And what is that, mango?" Patti asked.

"Very good. Yes, mango and pineapple."

"But neither of those is green," Ivy Mae said. She tentatively lifted the glass taking her first sip. After a moment, she nodded her head back and forth. "Okay, that's not so bad. It might not be my favorite, but it's not bad."

Iris laughed, "I think you have a mental block for any green drinks sister. I like it. What do you call it?"

"This is my Green Meanie."

"Not bad," Patti and Brenda agreed.

"I'd buy it," Zoey said.

"So, these two are protein smoothies. They are both low-calorie and could be a meal replacement. Do you think they will sell?"

"They'll sell. If I were you, I'd make sure the signage lists them as protein smoothies or meal replacements. That way folks won't be too surprised at the protein taste."

"Got it." Noah couldn't help but notice Ivy Mae passing the remainder of her green drink over to Iris.

"Not your favorite, Ivy Mae?" he asked.

"No, but that doesn't mean you shouldn't give it a shot."

"Alright, that's it for me tonight. Next."

Patty and Zoey looked at each other.

"Go ahead, Zoey."

"Alright, I'll go next." Zoey hopped up to run to the kitchen freezer. She came back a moment later. "Tonight, I have just one new flavor for you to try. But I'm really excited about it." Zoey scooped out bowlfuls of the frozen treat. She passed the bowls around the table, handed out the spoons and everyone started in.

"Oh, my goodness." Ivy Mae dug in for a second spoonful.

Iris laughed, "No offense Noah, but I do believe Ivy Mae prefers this ice cream to your smoothie."

"None taken. I'm familiar with Ivy Mae's preferences," Noah laughed. "Is this pistachio, Zoey?"

"Yes, this is a honey pistachio ice cream. I love the flavor combination. I'm quite happy with it."

"Oh, yes, I think you have a winner here," Brenda said scraping the last bit of ice cream from her bowl.

Patti looked around the table. "Can you imagine this in a warm waffle cone? I'd definitely buy it."

Zoey looked at Patti. "I think it's your turn to wrap the evening up."

"Alright folks, let's top off your evening with another sweet treat." She brought over two containers.

Ivy Mae leaned forward in her seat as Patti lifted the lid on the first container. Multiple oohs could be heard as she passed the container around the table. "I have two samples for you to try tonight. Both will be seasonal. The first one is a raspberry marble fudge which I plan to have available during raspberry season. It's a blend of white chocolate, bittersweet chocolate, and then the raspberry puree." Patti clasped her hands together as she looked around the table.

"Oh, my goodness." Zoey sat back in her chair and closed her eyes. "The tanginess of the raspberries offsets the sweetness of the white chocolate perfectly."

"I just know it's good," Ivy Mae commented.

Iris nodded her head in agreement.

"It's a winner," Brenda said.

Noah nodded. "Oh yeah, I agree. What else do you have?"

Patti lifted the lid off the other container revealing marbled red and white squares. "This one I call Red Velvet Christmas fudge. It'll be another seasonal treat."

Everyone agreed that she had two really good seasonal treats.

"Wow, that was sweet," Iris said.

"Can I get you ladies some coffee?" Brenda asked.

"Yes, please. Maybe decaf?"

"Coming right up."

Noah and Zoey poured some more smoothies into their glasses. Patti scooped a little more pasta salad onto her plate, while Brenda passed out the coffee cups.

Zoey looked over at the sisters, "So how goes the investigation?"

"The what?" Patti asked.

"Madam Sherlock over there is trying to solve Justin's murder," Noah said.

"You laugh, but I'm going to figure it out."

"Figure what out?" Brenda returned with a pot of coffee.

"Who killed Justin," Noah said matter of factly.

"So, who killed him?" Brenda asked.

Iris held her coffee cup up as Brenda poured her some coffee. "Don't encourage her."

Noah laughed out loud, "I don't think that would make any difference." Noah held up his drink to Ivy Mae. "Just be careful Ivy Mae, there's no telling who did him in."

"That's what I keep telling her. We've already received a threatening note."

Sara's coffee cup clanked on the table. "You what?"

Ivy Mae shushed her sister, but it was too late. The cat was out of the bag.

"It was nothing. The night after we had dinner with you, someone left a note in the door that's all."

"Why didn't you tell me?"

"Because, Sara, what good would it have done? It would have just made you worry." Ivy Mae shot her sister a look. "And I didn't want you to worry."

Noah looked at both ladies. "Did you at least report it to the sheriff?"

"No, she declined," Iris answered.

"Oh, good grief," Sara sighed.

"I'll watch out for her, Sara."

"Yeah, see I've got Iris to look out for me." Ivy Mae smiled broadly.

Sara just shook her head, clearly not convinced.

"If it makes you feel better Sara, I'll make sure the ladies get home safe tonight."

"Thanks Noah, that would make me feel better."

The group finally finished up and decided to call it a night.

"Well, this has been so much fun," Iris said. "Thank you so much for letting me join. Maybe next time, I can make something too."

"Of course, Iris. You're always welcome," Brenda told her.

Sara hugged her aunts. "I could come with you."

"No, I've got them. We'll be fine."

"Of course, we will. We'll talk to you later Sara. Good night everyone." The sisters drove home with Noah following behind in his car.

"Do you think this is really necessary?" Ivy Mae asked her sister.

"No, but it made Sara feel better. So, I'm willing to humor her."

As the three approached the front door, they could hear Daisy barking. Noah unlocked the door for the ladies and headed into the house ahead of them. They located Daisy bouncing up and down by the back door, barking like there was no tomorrow. Noah flipped the light switch, flooding the backyard in light.

Iris pointed, "What was that?"

"I don't see anything," Noah responded.

"Maybe it was just a shadow," Iris said.

Noah unlocked the door and stepped outside. Walking around the perimeter of the yard.

Ivy Mae looked at her sister, "That was no shadow. I saw it too."

"But I couldn't begin to tell who it was," Iris said.

"Me neither."

Daisy growled a bit more before she settled back down.

Noah returned, "It's all clear out there. Who knows, maybe Daisy was just barking at a squirrel."

"Probably," Ivy Mae responded. "She does have a thing for squirrels."

"You need anything else before I go?"

"No thank you, Noah," Iris responded. "We're fine. You go on now." Ivy Mae walked him to the front door and made sure she locked it behind him. She returned to the back door to find her sister staring out into the backyard.

"Whoever it was, hasn't come back. Shall we leave this light on tonight?"

"Yes. Did you double-check the door?"

"Yes, it's locked. We're safe and besides," Ivy Mae turned to the little pup curled up asleep on her bed, "if there was something out there, Daisy would let us know."

CHAPTER SIXTEEN

"THANKS. YES, THAT WOULD BE PERFECT." Ivy Mae hung up the phone, "Alright we each have appointments over at DeeDee's this morning.

"Thanks. I meant to get a haircut before I moved, but just didn't get around to it."

"Either way you'd have to get established with someone here."

"You're right. Is she any good?" Iris asked while sipping her morning tea.

"Of course, she is. Both ladies, DeeDee and Lola do an amazing job. I've never been disappointed with either of them. And it's also a great place to pick up the local news."

"Oh, now I understand. No wonder you're so eager to get a haircut."

Ivy Mae shrugged her shoulders and grinned, "You wouldn't want me to be uninformed on what's going on in my city, would you?"

"Of course not."

A short time later the sisters showed up at DeeDee's Do's.

DeeDee looked up when they walked in. "Have a seat ladies. We'll be finished in just a bit." DeeDee and her other hairstylists Lola were each working on other customers.

"No hurry, take your time," Ivy Mae said as she and her sister took a seat in the little waiting area.

Iris was glad Ivy Mae had spoken up because at the moment she wasn't sure she could. The faint smells of hair-spray and perm solution could be expected. But the colors on the walls took her by surprise. It was obvious that DeeDee had a thing for pink. The hair salon itself was a small narrow building, with the two longer walls were painted a bright shade of pink. The black and white tiles on the floor made Iris feel slightly dizzy. Thank goodness she was close to a chair in the little sitting area, although the zebra print fabrics didn't help her unsteadiness. A fuzzy black area rug, pink pillows in the chairs, and a black chandelier completed the look of the sitting area.

Iris wasn't sure what to think. She looked over at Ivy Mae the concern showing on her face. Ivy Mae gave her a satisfied grin before reaching to pick up a magazine.

Once Iris acclimated to her surroundings, she began to take note of the conversation around her. Lola was speaking with the client in her chair. "So, how's his mom doing?"

"Better now that she's had her surgery. Frank was so worried about her. He's been so stressed lately."

"I heard he had a couple of words with that guy who was killed," Lola said as she continued to snip at the woman's hair.

"You can say that again. He came home and told me all about it. Now I know my Frank has quite the temper. There's no doubt about that, but his mom and dad's health issues have just about pushed him over the edge. After we left the city council meeting the other night his dad called.

He said he was taking Frank's mom to the hospital and asked that we get there as soon as possible. I'm happy to say, she's doing so much better now."

"That's good to hear. I remember you brought her in here the last time she came to visit. She's a sweet lady."

"I'm just glad she's better because Frank gets cranky when he's stressed. And he's hard to deal with when he's grouchy."

Lola handed her customer a hand mirror. "Take a look at the back. Is that short enough?"

"Looks good."

Lola squirted some mousse into her hand and slathered it into the woman's short hair. She picked up the hairdryer and began to style her hair. The ladies continued to talk, but Iris couldn't hear their conversation any longer. Iris leaned over at her sister and whispered. "Did you hear that?"

"Of course, I did," Ivy Mae mumbled.

A little while later Ivy Mae found herself seated in DeeDee's chair with Iris seated in Lola's.

"How's business these days?" Ivy Mae asked.

DeeDee stopped combing and sighed. "We've actually been a little slow this week. You know I was almost hopin' those condos would be built. My business sure could have used a boost. I know that's not a very popular position these days with some of the folks in town."

"I can understand. You have a business to think about."

Her forehead wrinkled as she started working. "Most of the shop owners on Main Street don't understand. I mean, they get business from the tourists and weekend traffic. But no one's gonna come get their haircut while they're here for a weekend."

"Never thought about it that way, but you're right," Iris joined the conversation.

Lola quit cutting for a moment, "But you have to be careful about what you say and who you say it to, especially these days. It's turned into a very volatile issue for some people here in town."

"We had Cora in here the other day. Lord have mercy, she was madder than a cat getting baptized," DeeDee said with a snort.

Lola picked up the story where DeeDee left off. "Goodness, you should have heard her. She was so angry with Justin. She said he had confronted her on the street, getting all up in her face. She said Charlie had come up and tried to get him to leave her alone."

Ivy Mae had to remember not to moved her head, "Hmmph, I wonder how that turned out?"

Lola and DeeDee both stopped cutting the ladies' hair for a moment, looking at their customers in the mirror.

"Well as you can imagine, Charlie blew a gasket. But Justin ended up knocking him down," Lola said.

"Wow, we hadn't heard that," Iris said.

Deedee started combing through Ivy Mae's damp hair again. "Course a strong wind might do that, Charlies a bit scrawny. But let me tell ya, it's a good thing that boy didn't throw no punches. He's been in trouble with the law before."

"Oh?" Ivy Mae asked.

"Not here. His mom sent him here to live with his Uncle Norman. She thought he could use a man's influence."

"That one man caused so much dissension here, didn't he? Now I wonder what's going to happen. Does his death put an end to the condo project?" Iris looked over at Ivy Mae in the mirror, knowing she had asked a good question.

Lola shrugged her shoulders, "We just don't know yet. I suppose we'll have to wait and see."

Their conversation drifted to other topics and in no time the ladies had their hair cut and styled. As they stepped outside Ivy Mae looked over at her sister. "So, what do you think? Are you happy with your haircut?"

"Definitely. I wasn't sure what to make of that interior when I walked in, but DeeDee and Lola seem really nice. I like them both."

"I knew you would," Ivy Mae grinned. "So, what do you say, do you feel like making some cookies?"

"Oatmeal raisin?" Iris asked

"Or peanut butter."

"Since when do you make peanut butter cookies? They're not your favorite."

Ivy Mae raised one eyebrow. "I don't make the cookies for me. I take them over to the sheriff's office. Just sort of a thank you for your service."

Iris shook her head from side to side ever so slightly. "Or do you take them over as an opportunity to snoop?"

"Me? Snoop?" Ivy Mae opened her car door and climbed in, "Of course not. I actually take them a batch of cookies about twice a month or so. So, what do you say?"

"Of course, I'll help."

Fairly soon both ladies were up to their elbows in flour, sugar, and butter. They put two cookie sheets in the oven and settled down to have a cup of tea. Ivy Mae chose Chamomile tea while Iris made herself a cup of lemon hibiscus.

Ivy Mae sat quietly, sipping her tea and staring into space. Iris finally spoke up, knowing what was on her sister's mind. "So, it sounds like Frank has an alibi for the night of the murder."

Ivy Mae set her teacup down, "Yes. I'm fairly sure I can cross him off my list of suspects."

"Who does that leave you?"

"Cora, although I can't see that sweet thing shooting anyone."

Iris interrupted her, "Sister, people can do crazy things in the heat of the moment. Those two have definitely had their run-ins. And then there's Audrey, aka Miss I don't want my view blocked."

Easy laughter rang out from Ivy Mae. "I sure can't imagine shooting someone over a view, can you?"

"No, but you never know. Who else is there?"

Ivy Mae took a moment before she spoke, "Well, since we ruled Frank out. That only leaves Norman. And let's not forget, he reported his gun stolen."

"What, do you think he shot him and then reported his gun stolen? If he actually did shoot him, wouldn't it have been smarter to just throw the gun away somewhere? Why report it missing?"

The oven timer dinged and Ivy Mae hopped up. "Maybe to make himself look innocent," she shrugged walking back into the kitchen.

Thirty minutes later the ladies had two containers of cookies boxed up and ready to go. Their first stop was at the sheriff's office.

"Keep your eyes and ears, open sister," Ivy Mae said as they stepped out of the car.

"Of course, that goes without saying."

The two ladies entered the sheriff's office through the glass front door. Iris practically ran into her sister who stopped abruptly. "Ivy Mae, what are you doing?"

"Sorry sister," Ivy Mae continued on into the building.

"Good afternoon ladies." Officer Randall Blake looked

up from the open wide window that overlooked the lobby. He set down his pen and pushed some paperwork aside. "Ivy Mae, is that what I think it is?"

"Why yes, it is." Ivy Mae held out the container of cookies to the deputy. "I hope you and the guys enjoy them." Ivy Mae shook her finger at the detective, "Now don't you forget to share those."

The deputy laughed, crinkles forming at the corners of his eyes, "Don't I always?"

"I heard different last time I brought some over." Ivy Mae glanced around the lobby. "So, when did this wall go up?"

"Maybe about two or three weeks ago. Oh, you know, it just gives the guys a little privacy when they're working in the back."

Ivy Mae leaned a little closer to the deputy and whispered, "Any progress on the Cox case? I heard Norman reported his gun stolen."

"He did."

"You know we saw the incident between Justin and Frank the night Justin was shot, but we just heard Frank wasn't even in town that night. Do you have any other suspects?"

The deputy grinned back at her. "Ivy Mae, you know the sheriff would have my hide if I told you anything else about that case."

"Can't blame a lady for trying," she laughed. "Alright you enjoy the cookies and we'll talk later."

Iris followed her sister back to the car. "So, I take it that wall is new?"

"Yes, it used to be all open. Last time I was in, I could walk right up to where each deputy's desk."

"They may have done that as a safety issue. You know

times aren't like they used to be. You can't be too careful these days."

"Yes, but it makes it harder for me to get any new information. Darn it."

Iris grinned at her sister, "Come on, let's go. We have one more stop to make."

CHAPTER SEVENTEEN

IVY MAE PULLED her car into the botanical garden parking lot. Iris carried the tin of cookies and they pulled out their annual passes and entered through the front gates. A few minutes later one of the other gardeners told them where to find Ruby. It didn't take long before they spotted Ruby by one of the greenhouses.

"Yoo-hoo!" Ivy Mae called out. "We brought something for you guys here."

Ruby spotted the tin, "You've made my morning." She lifted the lid, lowered her head, and inhaled deeply. The fragrance of warm peanut butter was enough to make her mouth water. "Oh, my goodness, these smell so good. I'll put them in the break room...after I have one or two that is." She reached in and lifted out a cookie before closing the lid. The edges were crunchy, but the middle was soft, just like she liked them. "Thanks for these. What are you ladies up to today?"

"Cookie delivering," Iris responded.

Ivy Mae leaned closer to Ruby, "We found out this morning that Frank has an alibi, so I've crossed him off my list of suspects. We also heard Norman called in to report his gun stolen. We made a stop by the sheriff's office, but I'm afraid we didn't find out anything new."

"Until recently, I didn't even know Norman had a gun," Ruby said.

"Are those cookies?"

All three ladies turned to see Charlies, eyeing the cookie container.

"Yes, they are. Here you want to take them over to the break room for me?"

Charlie reached out for the container. "Sure, happy to."

The ladies waited until he was a way down the path before continuing their conversation. This also gave Ruby time to polish off the extra cookie she took out of the container before handing them over to Charlie.

"Those were as good as ever. Thanks again for the cookies. I'll have to get back over to the break room soon before they're all gone so I can snag another one."

"So, has he been acting weird?" Ivy Mae asked looking at Ruby.

"Who?"

"Norman, of course. Has he been acting out of the ordinary? I would imagine if you shot someone, there would be some telltale signs."

"Well now that you mention it, he seems quieter. You know like he's got something on his mind. Somethings bothering him. I tried talking to him, but he's not the chatty sort. So really, I have no idea what's going on with him." Ruby shrugged, "It could be just about anything."

"Keep your eyes and ears open for me, okay?"

"I always do," Ruby said before looking over at Iris. "Ivy Mae tells me you'd like to learn about gardening."

"Yes, it's something I have been interested in for a while now. Do you have volunteer opportunities here?"

"We sure do. Are you interested?"

Iris happily nodded, "Yes, just tell me when to show up."

"How about tomorrow?"

"I'll be here."

Ruby looked over at Ivy Mae. "Will we see you here too?"

"Not tomorrow. I think I have some other work to do tomorrow."

"No problem. Iris, dress comfortably, bring a hat, and plan to get dirty."

Ivy Mae and Iris said their goodbyes to Ruby and headed back to the parking lot. When they were back in the car, Iris looked over at her sister. "What are you going to be doing tomorrow?"

"Oh, you know, this and that. Maybe checking with a person or two about what they might know."

"Promise me you'll be careful."

"I'm always careful. Now, what do you say about a little linner?"

Iris laughed, "I haven't heard that term in so long."

"I think that was mother's favorite term, especially on the weekends when she didn't want to cook. Is Skipper's okay with you?"

"Perfect."

Ivy Mae headed to the edge of town and pulled into the dockside restaurant.

"Hello ladies," Francis hopped up from a table and welcomed them into the restaurant. There was only one other table occupied, probably due to the time of day. "Sit anywhere you like and here you go," Francis handed them each a menu. "Can I get you some tea?"

"Yes, please," the sisters responded at the same time.

By the time Francis came back with their drinks, both ladies had decided to get a grilled shrimp po'boy with a side of fries. They didn't have to wait long before Francis came back with their food. Whole wheat buns packed with glazed spicy shrimp, purple cabbage, sliced red onions, and tomatoes. They split the fries and settled in.

"Enjoy ladies," Francis said, taking the serving tray away. She returned to the dining room a few minutes later with a cup of coffee. She started to sit down at a table that gave her a view of the front door. Iris looked over at her sister and nodded her head toward Francis. Ivy Mae leaned around her sister.

"Francis, why don't you bring your coffee over here and visit with us."

"I'd love to."

Francis pulled up a chair at their table.

"It's kind of quiet in here today," Iris said.

"Just wait a couple of hours. It'll pick up."

Ivy Mae looked over at her, "So tell me, how do you feel about those condos?"

Francis raised her eyebrows and shook her head slightly. "Now that's a can of worms, isn't it. We could use the business, but I'm not sure I want the business if it's going to ruin the wildlife refuge. It's a real sticky issue that's for sure."

"It sure is. I've never seen this town so riled up."

Francis sipped her coffee. "I assumed that the condos were no longer going to be built."

"That very well could be. I hadn't heard some way or another."

Iris knew her sister was fishing for any information she

could get. "All I know is this is probably the best shrimp po'boy I've ever had."

Francis beamed, "That comes from getting them really fresh."

"And my special glaze," Dennis poked his head around the corner. "Hello, ladies."

Ivy Mae waved him over. "Dennis, come on in. Pull up a chair."

"Don't mind if I do."

"I'll getcha a cup of coffee, old man."

"Who are you calling an old man?"

Francis laughed as she walked away.

"We were just talking to Francis about the condos," Ivy Mae said.

"Good gravy, I'll be glad when that mess is over," Dennis huffed. "Some folks are so worked up about it." Francis returned with the cup of coffee for her husband.

Iris looked over at the man. "So, you're not worried about losing some business that you would have gained if the project had gone through."

"Ah, I ain't got time for what might have been. Folks around here know our food. I just rely on them to keep us afloat." He took a sip of his coffee. "And me and the guys are plenty busy in that kitchen."

Ivy Mae held up her last tiny bite of sandwich. "And this po'boy is incredible."

"I'm glad you like it." Dennis smiled proudly. "You ladies want some dessert?"

Iris and Ivy Mae looked at each other, grinned, and replied, "Cobbler, please."

"Cobbler it is." Francis hopped up, patting her husband on the shoulder. "You sit there and rest, I'll get it."

"Well of course you will. You're the waitress, not me."

"You trust me in your kitchen?" Francis teased her husband. After Francis rounded the corner, Dennis turned to the ladies. "She's one fantastic woman. I'd never be able to run this place without her."

A few minutes later Francis returned with two oversized portions of cobbler topped with vanilla ice cream melting into the warm cobbler.

"That's fresh. I just pulled it out of the oven a few minutes ago," Dennis grinned.

"And the ice cream comes from Zoey. She makes the best ice cream around."

"I've only had it once so far, but I think I agree with you," Iris said

Ivy Mae dug her spoon into the flaky crust. The juice of the berries and the melted ice cream puddled on her spoon. "Oh boy. This is so good," Ivy Mae said after her first bite.

Dennis looked over at Francis, "I think they like it."

"Looks that way."

"I gotta get back into the kitchen. Ladies thanks for coming in. Enjoy that dessert." Dennis stooped down and planted a kiss on his wife's forehead before heading off.

Francis sipped her coffee while the other ladies relished their desserts.

"I don't think I've ever had a better cobbler," Iris said. "This is the perfect topper to our meal, that's for sure."

"Isn't it though? I think you gave us an extra-large portion, but I'm not complaining," Iris said scooping up another spoonful of her cobbler.

About that time another group of customers entered and Francis got up to attend to them. A few minutes later she came by their table just to check on them. "Can I get you ladies anything else?"

"I think we've had more than enough," Ivy Mae sat back in her seat and blew out a breath.

Iris pulled out her card to pay their bill. "You know one of these days, we should order cobbler to go. Wonder if we could order like a nine-by-nine pan size?"

"We can make whatever size you'd like," Francis said as she came back by. "Just give us a call and we'll make you one special. Would you like two more servings to go, today?"

"Heavens no," Iris laughed. "I can't even think about any more food, but it's good to know for future reference."

The sisters grinned at each other and nodded. Ten minutes later they were climbing the steps into their little cottage.

"After all that food, I need a nap," Ivy Mae said "But if I take a nap now, I'll never sleep tonight."

"I know that's true. Let's go watch some birds."

Before long the sun dipped in the sky and the Ivy Mae went into the kitchen to make some tea for her and her sister.

Iris leaned her head back on the chair cushion and closed her eyes. The crashing sound of glass breaking shattered the quiet. Iris's eyes popped open as she sat up all of a sudden. "Ivy Mae!" she yelled hopping to her feet. "Are you okay?" By the time Iris made it into the kitchen she caught sight of Ivy Mae hurrying towards the front door.

CHAPTER EIGHTEEN

IVY MAE POINTED toward the front of the house. "It was something this way."

Daisy was hopping up and down, barking in the direction of the living room. The ladies rounded the corner into the living room hand in hand. They flipped the lights on and found a large round rock laying smack in the middle of the floor. An unwelcome breeze blew through one of the front nine-over-nine windows, bringing with it the normally calming scent of jasmine. Tonight, it had the opposite effect. They both stood frozen in their tracks, staring at the rock like it might sprout legs and run around. A moment later they came out of their daze. Ivy Mae stepped forward to scoop up the little dog who continued to growl. A note was rubber banded to the rock. Iris stepped forward to pick it up, her shoes, crunching on the shards of glass. She slipped the band off the rock and uncurled the scrap of paper.

"It says, stop asking questions, or you'll be sorry." She handed the note to Ivy Mae.

Ivy Mae studied the note, not wanting to believe what it said. "Oh Iris, this is bad."

Iris turned, headed into the other room.

'Where are you going?" Ivy Mae called after her sister.

"I need to get my phone. We need to call the sheriff."

"I don't know."

"What do you mean, you don't know?"

Ivy Mae shrugged and continued to stroke Daisy's fur possibly for comfort. "What can they do?"

"He needs to know," the volume of Iris's voice rose at her sister's comments. She pulled her phone from the table where she left it and dialed the sheriff. Iris ushered her sister to a seat at the dining room table. Ivy Mae seemed a bit stunned. Iris went to get a broom and dustpan until Ivy Mae hopped up coming out of her daze. She set Daisy down in the chair she had just vacated.

"The nerve!" Ivy Mae clenched her fists at her sides. "How dare they, think they can intimidate me."

"Well, they intimidated me," Iris snapped back.

Ivy Mae took the broom from her sister. "We should probably sweep that after they see the room. If that matters."

The reflection of red and blue flashing lights could be seen on the walls of the home. The ladies headed toward the front door in response to the pounding.

"Ivy Mae, Iris are you okay?"

The sisters flipped on the porch light to see Deputy Randall Blake standing there.

"Oh, I'm glad it's you, deputy."

They ushered him in and his eyes swept the room in a matter of moments.

"Are you ladies alright? You're not hurt, are you?"

"No, we're fine, just shaken up a bit, I suppose," Iris responded.

"I was shaken up, now I'm just angry. Look what someone did to my front window. Ugh. I'm not even sure I can get anyone out here tonight to get that fixed," Ivy Mae huffed.

"No probably not. So, was it a rock?"

"Yes, it's in here, along with the note."

"Note?" The deputy followed the two ladies into the other room.

"Deputy would you like a cup of tea?"

"No Iris, I'm fine, thank you."

"Here's the note." Ivy Mae handed him the piece of paper.

The deputy read the note, flipped the paper over, and read it again. He dropped it on the table and looked over at Ivy Mae.

"Is there anything you want to tell me?"

"No," Ivy Mae mumbled.

Iris came back into the room, setting a cup of tea in front of her sister.

"Well, Ivy Mae, I know the sheriff says you sometimes get involved in his investigations." He held the note up. "You've ruffled someone's feathers. Any idea who?"

Ivy Mae and Iris looked at each other. "I mean granted I've talked to some folks in town about the murder, but I don't think I've upset anyone."

Iris spoke up, "I agree. I haven't heard of anything from anyone. Definitely no threats. No one we've talked to has even been close to doing something like this."

"Unfortunately, some folks may not appear upset when they really are. Obviously, ladies, people can be very deceptive. I need you to know, if someone could do this, then they could step it up. Is there anywhere you ladies could go spend the night?"

Ivy Mae slapped the tabletop. "We aren't leaving! We won't be forced out of our house."

"I agree with Ivy Mae. We'll stay here tonight. We'll be safe. We just need to see if we can get that window patched."

The radio the deputy wore squawked and the deputy stepped into the other room to answer.

"Thanks for backing me up. I really do believe we'll be fine. We have Daisy here to protect us too." The little dog raised her head, stretching before giving the ladies a wide yawn.

Iris turned to her sister with one eyebrow raised. "That little ball of fluff?"

"Now, sister, don't hurt her feelings."

Iris pressed her lips together and shook her head. "Do you have any plywood?" Iris asked. "We could at least cover the hole for now."

"No, I don't think I do. I'm sure I can find cardboard though." Ivy Mae hopped up, "Let me go find something."

"I'll get the tape."

When the ladies got back into the living room, they heard the front door open. "Hey, Chief."

"Randall. They doing okay?"

Ivy Mae hesitated as she entered the room cardboard in one hand and Daisy under her other arm. "Yes, we're fine. Just a little startled and quite frankly annoyed. "Who would do this?"

Sheriff McGuire pushed back his hat, "Well Ivy Mae, you've evidently gotten a little too close to a killer. You probably didn't even notice. Who have you been talking to?"

"Just friends. Really."

The sheriff looked between the woman and the window. "Let me get this fixed and I'll be right back."

Iris reached for the broom. Daisy squirmed in Ivy Mae's arms and ran from the room, once Ivy Mae set her down. Daisy wasn't a fan of a broom or vacuum. The sheriff headed back out to his car and brought back a hunk of plywood and drill. A few minutes later the sheriff and deputy had the hole covered, while the ladies swept up the glass. The men returned and Ivy Mae wasn't sure she was ready for the conversation she knew was coming.

"Good night ladies. Call if you need anything else. Deputy Blake dipped his hat at the ladies before nodding at his boss. "Sheriff."

Iris closed the door after the deputy left. "Sheriff, would you like a cup of coffee?"

"Yes, please. That would be appreciated."

Ivy Mae and the sheriff made their way into the dining room.

"Can I see the note?" The dining room chair creaked under his weight.

Ivy Mae reached across the table to retrieve the note. *Here we go* Ivy Mae thought to herself. She knew she was in for a lecture.

The sheriff looked the note over carefully. He sighed heavily, took his hat off, and leaned over to Ivy Mae. "You know I may sound a little stern with you sometimes, but it's only because I want you to stay safe. I would hate for anything to happen to you. It's one thing for someone to come after me, it's my job. I was hired to keep the peace and hunt down criminals. It's my job, not yours."

Iris brought the sheriff's coffee in. "We really haven't been talking to anyone who I could ever imagine doing this. I mean I may be new to Blue Water Bay, but I can't image

Francis or Dennis or Ruby or the ladies over at the beauty shop tossing a rock through our window. Much less attaching a threatening note to it."

"And it might not have been one of them, but someone has obviously heard or seen you asking questions." The sheriff held his hands out, "Otherwise this wouldn't have happened." He looked back and forth between the two ladies.

The sisters looked at each other. "I can't think of anyone. We really haven't found any good information. Honestly, I've ruled out people more than anything."

"Oh?" the sheriff's eyebrows rose. "Who have you ruled out?"

"Frank for one. Iris and I saw a couple of run-ins between him and Justin."

"And how did you happen to rule out Frank?" the sheriff grinned.

Iris pipped up, "We got our hair cut."

A grin crossed the sheriff's face, "Well that makes perfect sense."

"She's right we went to DeeDee's and Frank's wife was there. We just listened to her talk and she mentioned that Frank went out of town following the town council meeting."

"His mom was sick," Iris added.

"Anyone else?"

The ladies looked at each other again before Ivy Mae spoke up. "Well, there's Cora. We know they didn't get along."

"Uh-huh."

Ivy Mae shrugged, I haven't talked to her too much, but she seems so sweet. She surely couldn't have shot that man, no matter how much he pushed her buttons."

"Did you see any exchanges between the two? I mean anything out of the ordinary."

"I did," Iris spoke up. "That day I came to town, right before my accident. They were toe to toe out there on the sidewalk. Cora and her team were picketing out there and he walked by."

"Look ladies, people wear masks. They pretend to be a lot of things. Are you familiar with some serial killers? They seem like normal, everyday people. No one ever suspects them of anything." He paused to sip his coffee. "You need to stop asking questions." He looked from one to the other. "Promise me to you'll behave and stay out of my business. Understand?"

"Yes," they both mumbled.

He took another sip of coffee and reached for his hat. "I better be going. Call if you have any other problems, you hear me?"

Iris stood up to walk him out, "I'm sure we'll be fine."

They started walking to the front door.

"Although we haven't done anything wrong," Ivy Mae mumbled.

"I heard that Ivy Mae," the sheriff called out from the other room.

CHAPTER NINETEEN

"GOOD MORNING," Ivy Mae covered a yawn. "How did you sleep last night?"

"Not very well, at least initially." Iris was dressed and ready for her day at the garden. "Go sit down and I'll bring you something. Coffee or tea?"

"Maybe coffee."

Ivy Mae took her seat at the table in the sunroom. It was bright and sunny out. The birds chirped as they hopped around one of the birdbaths in the back garden. Things looked so cheery this morning in comparison to the threatening events of the night before.

"Here's your coffee."

"Thank you, sister." Ivy Mae took a sip of her coffee, closed her eyes for a moment. "Oh, that is so good. Are you ready for your day at the garden?"

"Yes," Iris hesitated, "But I'm not sure I want to leave you here. Why don't you come with me?"

"Don't worry about me. I'll be fine. And besides, I need to call someone to get the window repaired."

"It will be nice to get that taken care of. You just be careful today."

"Oh, I will, but don't you think if whoever threw that rock really wanted to hurt us, they wouldn't have stopped with just throwing a rock?"

"Huh, guess I hadn't thought about it like that, but maybe they were just getting started."

Ivy Mae reached over and patted her sister's hand, "I'll be fine. Don't worry. Now, what would you like for dinner tonight? I have a few errands to run, but I'll be home in plenty of time to cook something yummy tonight."

"Errands? What kind of errands?"

Ivy Mae pressed her lips together and set her coffee cup down. "If you must know I thought I'd pay a visit on Audrey."

"Did you not learn anything from last night? Surely, you didn't forget about that rock that came flying through the window?"

"Of course not, but the sooner we figure this out, the better we'll be."

Iris threw her hands in the air. "I give up. If you're going to snoop, you have to be more discreet, because you've obviously gotten someone's attention."

"You're right. I need to be more sleuthy. Sleuthier? Oh, whatever, you know what I mean."

Iris took her last sip of coffee. "Is there anything you need me to do today?"

"Keep your eyes and ears open. I don't know if you can, but go back to the scene of the crime and see if we missed anything."

"I'll do my best. You keep your phone handy. I'll check on you from time to time."

"Roger that," Ivy Mae said clapping her hands together. "I love having you as a partner in crime."

Iris rolled her eyes, grabbed her backpack, snapped on her tricycle helmet, and headed out. Ivy Mae pulled her phone and called a glass repairman. While she waited, she began to make notes about the case and her suspects. Before long the repairman was there and her new window installed.

"I'm sorry, not this time girl?" Ivy Mae made sure the pup had fresh water and a full bowl before leaving on her morning jaunt. She drove up the hill and down the road that led to Audrey's house. *Well here goes,* Ivy Mae thought to herself. Was there anything she was actually going to be able to learn today? This was definitely a bold move on Ivy Mae's part. Hopefully, it would be fruitful too.

She exited the car and walked boldly up to Audrey's front door. Ivy Mae rang the bell and didn't have to wait long before Audrey answered the front door.

"Hello?"

Ivy Mae thought she looked just as put together this morning as she did the evening of the council meeting. "Yes, hello. My name is Ivy Mae. I just wanted to say I appreciated your impassioned speech you gave the other night at the town council meeting."

The door opened a little wider, "Thank you. Would you like to come in?"

"I'd love to."

"Why don't we go sit out on the patio. I'll show you my view of the ocean."

"Yes, that would be lovely."

Audrey escorted Ivy Mae through the sleek modern home. Shiny surfaces and sharp corners filled the house. The house was spotless and didn't look lived in at all.

"Your house is very pretty."

"Thank you," Audrey responded. "You'll have to excuse the mess. My cleaning lady hasn't been here yet this week."

A frown flitted briefly across Ivy Mae's face. She didn't see anything out of place, much less any pesky dust.

"Here we go," Audrey said sliding open the glass patio doors.

Ivy Mae's breath caught in her throat. "Oh, I see what you mean. You have a glorious view, don't you?" The wide expanse of the crystal blue ocean spread out before her. Ivy Mae inhaled catching the scent of the saltwater. She could hear the waves pounding on the rocky shore below.

"Can I get you something to drink?"

"Oh, no. I wouldn't want to trouble you."

"No trouble. Maybe a cup of tea?"

"Yes, that would be nice."

"Why don't you have a seat at the table and I'll be right back."

Audrey had a beautifully landscaped backyard and patio. Large glazed pots with cascading blossoms tastefully decorated the corners of the patio. A table set on the cover with fans spinning slowly overhead.

"Here we go." She brought the tea and a sparkling water for herself.

"Thank you so much, I appreciate your time. This view is amazing."

"You can see why I was so passionate about that dreadful condo complex. It would totally destroy my view and the whole feel out here."

"But didn't you ever worry about someone building down there?"

Audrey shrugged, "No, not at all. When I bought the

property, I was advised that no one could build on it, because of the botanical garden and the wildlife preserve.

"So, you can see the botanical garden?"

"Come with me, I'll show you." Audrey walked Ivy Mae to the edge of her property. "See, that's the trail down there." Audrey pointed. "Follow it along, it comes right down here in front of my property and continues on to the border of the botanical garden."

"And this little section down there is where they wanted to build the condos?"

"Yes, that's it. Right smack in front of my property. The two ladies stood together in the backyard. "Can you imagine what it would look like to have a building there? Depending on how many floors it has, my property could be eye level to someone's front door. I would never have any privacy. And to make it worse, I'd lose that absolutely magnificent view."

"I suppose you know Justin Cox was killed just down the trail that way."

"Yes, I heard about it on the news. It's creepy to know that someone might have walked down that trail right below my house." Audrey shuddered and stood silent for a moment before responding quieter than normal. "I've always felt safe here at home. Now? Not so much."

"I'm sure you don't have anything to worry about. Do you by any chance have a security system with cameras?"

"Yes, but if you're wondering, they only show the yard, nothing down the hill. And it's so dark down there at night."

"I suppose the sheriff has questioned you about where you were that night."

"Yes, he did. I was actually shocked when he stopped by to talk to me. I mean can you imagine, me? Who could possibly think I killed that man? But on the other hand, I didn't have a good response for him either. I didn't have anyone who could confirm my alibi." Audrey shrugged sipping her water, "I left the council meeting with the beginnings of a migraine. After I got home, I took some medication and went straight to bed."

"I'm sure he was just covering his bases, but you do have a lot to lose if those condos are built."

"I did have a lot to lose," Audrey corrected with a smile.

"What do you mean?"

"Let's just say I decided not to leave anything up to chance. I took matters into my own hands. You probably know I have parties here from time to time and over the years, I've gotten to meet some well-placed people. One of them put me in touch with someone Justin worked with and we discussed the project. In turn, I put them in touch with someone who has some coastal property they are looking to sell in the next town over." Audrey held her hands out palms up, "Voila, problem solved."

Ivy Mae sat in her chair quietly. Thoughts raced through her mind. That almost gave her more of a motive to have killed Justin. The cautionary words from her sister and the sheriff rang in her head.

"Well, I'm glad your view is safe," Ivy Mae said raising her teacup to the woman. "Thank you so much for letting me barge in today this morning." Ivy Mae stood up from her seat and took one more look at the wide expanse of the ocean. "That really is incredible. I think I could look at that view all day long."

"Of course. Maybe you and your sister could come to one of my next parties."

"My sister?"

"Yes, I heard she moved back to town. I bet you're so happy to have her back."

"I am. I didn't know you knew my sister had moved

back to town." Ivy Mae laughed, trying to shake off her uneasy feelings, "You do get around."

"Oh, there's not much that goes on in Blue Water Bay that I don't know about," Audrey laughed.

Ivy Mae laughed. She tried to shake off the uneasy feeling as Audrey walked her to the door. She couldn't wait to tell Iris about the conversation she had with Audrey.

CHAPTER TWENTY

IVY MAE TURNED her little car toward the botanical garden. She wasn't certain what to make out of her conversation with Audrey. For whatever reason, the last couple of comments from the woman made Ivy Mae uneasy. Was Audrey trying to discover what Ivy Mae knew? Maybe Audrey wasn't guilty. Maybe she let her into her home, to talk to her to see what she knew. It was obvious Audrey liked knowing what was going on in town. Ivy Mae shook her head as these thoughts ran through her head. Maybe she was just overly anxious because of the incident the prior evening.

The familiar sound of the gravel crunched under Ivy Mae's feet as she headed down one of the paths in the garden. She was told Iris was down this direction. She rounded the corner past the conifer collection and spotted Arthur sitting on his regular bench. His newsboy cap perched on his head and his umbrella leaned against the bench. Surprisingly today though his newspaper was folded in his lap and he was actually carrying on a conversation. She recalled the many times she had initiated a conversation with the man with minimal results and mainly grunts. But today he seemed to be in a lively conversation with of all people, her sister, Iris. Ivy Mae didn't know whether she should approach them or walk away. She sure didn't want to send Arthur back into his shell. But the decision was made for her.

Iris looked up and noticed her sister down the path. "Ivy Mae come over and have a seat. Arthur was telling me the most fascinating story."

"Oh, I don't know how fascinating it was," Arthur chuckled. "I was just telling her a little about my past career."

"Arthur here is retired from the US Marshal service. Can you imagine?"

Ivy Mae tried not to show her surprise. "That sounds incredible. I'll bet you do have some stories to tell."

"Here you go," Arthur scooted over on the bench. "Have a seat, won't you?"

"Thank you." Ivy Mae gratefully took the seat on the bench that he offered to her. This man had never been chatty before. What in the world was going on?

Iris looked at her sister and continued hesitantly, "The sheriff was here this morning. When he saw me, he asked how we did last night. Arthur overheard us talking and anyway one thing led to another. After the sheriff left, he called me over and I told him about the present that came flying through our window last night."

"Yes, it wasn't anything we expected that's for sure."

"I'm pleased that neither of you were injured." He looked back and forth between the two of them as he cleaned his glasses. "And you didn't see anyone outside?"

Ivy Mae's shoulder's sagged, "No unfortunately or fortunately we both were in the back of the house."

"Honestly I didn't even think about looking out front," Iris said.

"Well, I can imagine that it wouldn't have been the first thing on your mind."

Ivy Mae looked over at him, "So I'm sure you are aware of the murder of Justin here in the garden?"

Arthur kept cleaning his glasses before returning them to his prominent nose. "Of course. Any idea who did it?" Arthur asked looking directly at Ivy Mae.

"Why would you ask that?"

A hearty laugh escaped from the man. "Because I see things, like the day Justin died. I watched you take that path that led right behind where the sheriff was talking to Norman and Charlie. But as I watched, you didn't come out on the other side." He shrugged as he grinned at Ivy Mae, "Wasn't that difficult to figure out what you were doing."

"Close your mouth sister," Iris grinned.

Ivy Mae looked back at her sister, "He's good."

Iris nodded in return. "Yes, he is."

"So, is there anything you can tell me about Justin's murder?"

"Unfortunately, no," Arthur sighed. "By the time I got here that morning, the police had already shown up. What do you know so far? Any suspects?'

"A few. And a few that I've been able to rule out."

"Start with the ones you've ruled out," Arthur urged Ivy Mae on.

"Frank, a local plumber. He had a couple of run-ins with the victim. But according to his wife he left town right after the town council meeting. Norman, one of the gardeners here reported his handgun missing. He also had a few choice words for Justin one morning, back by the rose bed. He spotted Justin pouring a cola on one of the rose-bushes, which if left unchecked could kill the roses."

"Granted it would probably take more than one dousing for that to happen," Iris added.

"But just the same, Norman was pretty upset with him." Ivy Mae looked at Iris, "Probably because some of the rose bushes back there were in sad shape already." Iris nodded in agreement.

Ivy Mae continued on. "I know he and Charlie were at the council meeting, but I have no idea if he has an alibi."

"I think I can help you there," Iris said holding up her hand. "I found out that he couldn't have been the killer."

"Oh, and why is that, sister?"

"I was talking to Ruby this morning, she told me she talked to Norman's girlfriend who said Norman was with her after the council meeting. Seems like they had started going out not too long ago."

"Think she was telling the truth?" Arthur asked.

Iris shrugged. "I have no idea, but Ruby seemed to think she was truthful."

"Well, I suppose we can scratch him off the list," Ivy Mae said while staring out over the garden.

Iris was familiar with that look. The wheels in her sister's head were spinning. "How did it go with Audrey?"

Arthur turned to Ivy Mae. "Audrey? I heard she was concerned with the condos blocking her view. Sounds like a motive to me."

"Honestly, she did make me feel a little leery. She told me she developed a migraine following the meeting. She said she took some medication after she got home and went straight to bed."

"So, what made you uncomfortable?"

Ivy Mae looked over at Iris, "She knew you were back in

town. I wasn't even aware that she knew I had a sister, much less that you had moved back here. She said there wasn't much in town that she didn't know about. I don't know, maybe it's nothing. Maybe that rock through the window last night has just made me jumpy."

Arthur huffed, shaking his head. "I'd be surprised if you weren't spooked. I mean it's not every day something like that happens to you."

"Thank goodness for that," Iris said.

"Guess that means I need to go pay a call on Cora."

"I'm supposed to be helping Ruby again this afternoon, but I can cancel if you'd like some company. I don't like the thought of you out there by yourself."

"Oh, sister I'll be fine. I see her in town a lot. I'm going to try to catch up with her in town."

"I'd volunteer to go with you, but I have an appointment this afternoon and I'm afraid I can't cancel," Arthur said.

"Thanks, for the offer, Arthur but that's alright." Ivy Mae glanced between Arthur and her sister noting the concern on their faces. Ivy Mae rolled her eyes at them, "Really? What? Do you think I'll get gunned down on Main Street? Don't worry, I'll be fine. But on another topic, one of these days Arthur, maybe you could tell us about your days as a US Marshall."

Arthur tipped his head, "I'd be delighted."

CHAPTER TWENTY-ONE

IVY MAE LEFT the botanical garden hopeful that she could run into Cora in town. The young woman always seems to be around somewhere. Ivy Mae parked her car in-between Main Street Creamery and Smoothie Goodness. As she looked up and down Main Street, she didn't spot Cora anywhere. *That would be too lucky*, she thought to herself.

She heard the little bell tinkle over the door of the Main Street Creamery. A mom and her two little children trooped happily out the door each licking the ice cream from their waffle cones. Maybe Zoey could point her in the right direction. Ivy Mae laughed, and if not, maybe she could get herself just a tiny ice cream cone.

"Hey Ivy Mae," Zoey's chipper voice called out. "Where's your sidekick?"

"She's over at the botanical garden. She's doing a little volunteer work over there."

"So, what are you up to today?"

"Oh, you know, this and that."

"Can I get you something?

"How about a single dip of your lemon cookie delight. It's been a while since I had that flavor."

"You got it."

She scooped large curls of ice cream, pressing them down into the waffle cone.

That was definitely more than a single scoop, Ivy Mae thought.

"Here you go," Zoey said handing it over.

"So, what's new?" Ivy Mae asked after paying for my treat.

"Not much. Anticipating for a delivery of fresh strawberries and peaches soon."

"Oh good, I love your peaches and cream ice cream."

"Thank you."

Ivy Mae stood there licking her ice cream cone. "So, heard anything new about Justin's murder?"

"No, I haven't heard anything. But it seems quieter around town now that...well you know. Maybe I should be asking you that question. You're the one who's always in the know."

"There is some news that the condo project is dead. Oh, maybe that was a poor choice of words. What I meant was I heard that the project will proceed in the next town over."

"Oh, wow. Where did you hear that?"

Ivy Mae grinned at the young woman. "I have my sources."

"I wonder if Cora has heard the good news. She'll be over the moon."

"I don't know, but I was sort of looking for her. Have you seen her today?"

"No, but you want me to call her for you? I'm sure she'd love to hear your news."

The little bell over the door rang and Ivy Mae turned to see Cora in the doorway.

"Well, speak of the devil," Zoey said with a grin.

Cora stopped in her tracks, "What? What did I do?"

"Nothing," Cora laughed. "Ivy Mae here has some good news for you."

"I could use some good news. Especially after this week."

"It is second-hand news, but I did hear the condominium project has moved to another town."

"Really?" Zoey's eyes lit up momentarily before she became wary again. "Do you believe your source? I mean, are they reliable?" A frown creased her forehead.

Ivy Mae took another couple of licks of her ice cream before responding. "Audrey told me."

"You mean Audrey Anderson, who spoke at the council meeting?" Zoey asked.

"Yes, I went to see her this morning. She told me she was in contact with someone at the firm where Justin worked. She told them she knew someone with some coastal property they wanted to sell and that was that. No more condos in Blue Water Bay." Ivy Mae continued to work her way through her creamy treat.

Excitement lit up Cora's eyes which darted back and forth between the other two ladies. "Really? Really? Eeeeee! I can't believe it. Mission accomplished. Wait until I tell everyone." Cora pressed her fists up to her mouth to stifle the squeals as she danced around in a circle. She stopped and looked back at Ivy Mae. "We won? We really won?"

"Well, I'm far from an official source, so don't get too excited."

Zoey laughed, "I think it's too late for that."

"I really hope you're right. That would be amazing." Her excitement seemed a little short-lived. "I do wish this could have ended peacefully though. I mean I wish Justin hadn't had to die." Zoey's, mouth fell open, "Wait that didn't come out right. What I meant was it's a shame that someone thought he had to die in order to stop the project."

"I'm sure by now the sheriff has spoken with you about Justin's murder."

"Yes, he has. No surprise there. Practically everyone in town knows what I thought about him. After folks heard he died the whispers and finger-pointing started. People think I did him in, can you imagine? Me?"

Ivy Mae eyed the young woman closely as she continued to work her way through her ice cream.

Zoey spoke up, "Don't pay any attention to them, Cora. Your true friends, people who know you wouldn't begin to think that about you. And besides, you have an alibi."

Ivy Mae watched the exchange between the two women in silence.

"Well, I suppose that depends on what time Justin was killed."

"Why? What do you mean?" Ivy Mae asked crunching on her waffle cone.

"Cora and I went out to eat after the meeting was over."

"Yes, I was so anxious before the meeting, I couldn't eat anything. So, after the meeting Cora and I went out and grabbed a bite."

"Then we went back to my house," Zoey said. "We opened a bottle of wine and binge-watched The Copper Ridge Mysteries."

Zoey picked up the narrative. "Of course, between the wine and the stress of the day, we only got to about the middle of the third episode before we fell asleep."

"I woke up about 3 a.m. I covered Cora up with a blanket and went to bed. It was so late, there was no point in waking her up."

"I know I didn't kill him and you know I didn't kill him, but some people would say, I wasn't really asleep. Or they'll think I left the house after you fell asleep or either left the house after you went to bed."

Zoey crossed her arms, "Stop that. I'm sure the sheriff will find out exactly what happened."

"Gosh, I sure do hope so. I'm tired of looks and whispers. I've thought about taking a vacation or visiting my family back east, just until things settle down a bit. But even that would look bad. People would think I'm on the run or something."

"Do either of you have any ideas of who could have killed Justin?" Ivy Mae asked. The crunch of the waffle cone seemed loud in the silence that followed.

Cora shrugged. "No. Maybe I'm just young and naive, but it's hard for me to imagine something like that even happening here in Blue Water Bay. Obviously, I didn't want the condos built, but I sure wasn't going to kill anyone to stop them."

"Maybe it was someone from Justin's life. You know someone who doesn't even live in Blue Water Bay. They come to town, kill him, hoping that someone in town would be incriminated," Zoey said.

"Oh, I hadn't thought about that. I wonder if Sheriff McGuire has considered that?"

"I have considered all sorts of things," a voice boomed behind the ladies, causing them to jump. Sheriff McGuire stood in the doorway. "Did you get your window repaired Ivy Mae?"

"Ya...yes, I did." Her heart was still pounding. Had they

been so wrapped up in the conversation they hadn't even heard the little bell? "You startled me."

"Maybe if you were minding your own business, you wouldn't have been so startled." The sheriff looked over at Zoey, "Can I get a pint of your banana pudding and then another pint of your blueberry pie flavor?"

"Sure thing." Zoey began working on the sheriff's order.

Cora took this moment to approach the sheriff. "Sheriff, is it true that the condo project is off?"

He shook his head, "I'm sorry Cora, at this point I'm not able to confirm that."

He looked between Cora and Ivy Mae, "Where did you hear this?"

Ivy Mae popped the last bite of waffle cone in her mouth and stood quietly.

"You know, word spreads in town." Cora tried to brush off the question, but the sheriff wasn't fooled.

He huffed in frustration. "Ivy Mae, where'd you hear this?"

Well, there was no denying it now. She might as well just get it over. She squared her shoulders and looked him directly in the eyes. "Audrey told me. She said she had a contact in Justin's company and they are now going to be building the condos in another town."

"You get around more than I could have imagined." The sheriff lifted his hat and scratched his head. "Maybe you should have been a deputy investigator."

"I'm sure I would have been good at it."

Sheriff McGuire admitted, "I'm sure you would have been."

Ivy Mae grinned proudly, if not a bit prematurely.

"But since you're not," the sheriff's voice rising, "I

would appreciate you staying out of this. Don't forget what happened last night."

"Here you go, sheriff." Zoey held up his order. He finished his transaction and turned to leave the shop

Cora spoke up, "What happened last night?"

The sheriff tipped his hat to the women, heading toward the door.

Ivy Mae crossed her arms and scowled. "Oh, you're such a blabbermouth."

The women could hear the sheriff chuckling as he walked out. Ivy Mae didn't have to look at the ladies to know they were staring at her. Zoey broke the silence. "Well? Are you going to tell us? What happened last night?"

Ivy Mae sighed heavily, "Someone threw a rock through our living room window last night."

Cora gasped, "What?"

"Oh, my goodness, Ivy Mae. Are you and Iris alright?"

"Why would someone do that?" Cora asked.

Ivy Mae held up her hands. "Yes, yes. We're fine. I suppose I've gotten a little too close to whoever killed Justin. There was a note attached to the rock. It said for me to stop asking questions."

"Ivy Mae! That's scary. I can see now why the sheriff was so upset about you poking about in this case." Zoey came from behind the counter and gave her friend a hug.

"Oh, now, now. It wasn't that bad," Ivy Mae patted her hand. "Don't fret. Iris and I are fine and Deputy Blake and the sheriff were there in no time at all."

"Just promise me you'll be careful."

"I'm always careful."

"Obviously not careful enough, otherwise you'd never had a rock sailing through your window," Cora responded.

"Don't worry about me, I'm a tough ole bird." Ivy Mae glanced at her watch, "Oh, it's later than I thought. Ladies, I'd love to stay and chat, but I've got to get home and get some dinner made. I promised Iris a good meal tonight."

They gave her a wave as she headed out the door.

CHAPTER TWENTY-TWO

IVY MAE WAS quiet as she sipped her tea the next morning. Thoughts of the murder swirled in her head. Had she ruled out a suspect prematurely? Could she have been mistaken about Cora? She appeared to be such a sweet young thing. Was there a suspect she missed?

Iris knew what was on her sister's mind. "You want to go with me this morning. We're going to be planting some flowers in a new summer bed?"

Ivy Mae sat for a moment staring over her teacup. "You know, I think will. It'd be fun to get out in the sun and work in the dirt a bit."

"I think it'd be good for you to get out and do something besides worrying over Justin's murder."

"Oh, now don't you start on me too. I got enough of that from the sheriff, Cora, and Zoey yesterday."

"You're right, I'm sorry." Iris sipped her tea. "I can understand why Audrey's comments unsettled you. But don't forget, Blue Water Bay is a small town. You know what the rumor mill is like here."

"Maybe you're right," Ivy Mae admitted. She stacked

their dishes after they finished eating and carried them into the kitchen. "I'm going to go get ready. Will you listen for Daisy to come back in?"

"Of course."

A short while later, Daisy was set for the day, and the sister headed to the garden on their tricycles. Pretty soon, they were working fertilizer into the dirt that would be the new flower bed. The sun sparkled and Ivy Mae felt the heat of the sun warming her shoulders. The longer she worked, the more the tension of the past few days faded away. This was exactly what she needed.

Further down the way, Charlie worked on a section of the garden where they were putting in a birdbath. He leveled the ground, tamping down the soil.

"Isn't this fun?" Iris asked.

"I will say working in the dirt is more relaxing than I thought it would be." Ivy Mae rubbed her cheek leaving a smudge of dirt. "And it feels so good out here today."

"How's it going ladies?" Ruby walked up, surveying the future flower bed.

Iris sat back on her heels. "I think we're ready to plant."

"Why don't you ladies take a break and I'll go get the plants. We'll meet back here in fifteen minutes or so."

"Sounds good to me," Ivy Mae said, peeling off her gloves. She stood up slowly, stretching her back and neck. "I think this bed is going to be quite lovely when we're finished."

"I agree. Come on, let's go get something to drink."

Iris and Ivy Mae walked down the sidewalk to the break room and helped themselves to some bottles of lemonade and a couple of cookies that they had brought in with them that morning. A few minutes later they got up from their seats, ready to get back at it.

"Hey look who's here," Iris said.

Arthur sat on the bench reading his newspaper. "Good morning ladies. A beautiful day isn't it?"

"Yes, it's glorious out here. I can see why you like coming here."

"Yes, I love to sit out here, soak up the sun, and read my paper. I find it very relaxing"

"We'll let you get back to it. Come on Ivy Mae, Ruby's probably waiting for us. We don't want to keep her waiting."

"Don't let me keep you, because you sure don't want to be late. Some folks on staff here seem kinda cranky today."

Ivy Mae cocked her head, "Oh? And who might that be?"

"Norman and Charlie. They were going at it a while ago."

"What in heavens about?"

Arthur folded his newspaper giving the women his full attention. "It seems like Charlie totally disregarded some instructions Norman gave him. Something about installing a birdbath. I don't really know."

"Oh, for crying out loud. Fussing over the placement of a birdbath?" Ivy Mae shook her head.

"Sounds like they're having a bad day," Iris said.

"Well, at least we're working with Ruby. Come on Iris, let's get back and get those flowers planted."

"Good seeing you Arthur." The sisters said their goodbyes and headed back to join Ruby.

She was already busy placing the pots out in the bed, arranging and rearranging their placement. They watched her until she was finished. Ruby finally stood back critically eyeing the placement of the pots.

"Okay, I think this is good. Let's start with the back

and we'll work our way forward." Each of the ladies took a pot and started in. Soon they had all the salvia planted. Ruby stood back and brushed off her hands. "These are going to look so pretty as they fill in. It's going to be a carpet of purple. Now let's get the dahlias and zinnias in."

"What colors will these be?" Iris asked.

"We have quite a variety. Everything from a dark pink petal with white tips, yellow petals with pink tips, peach color, yellow." Picking up another few pots she said, "and let's not forget the orange ones with white tips. And that's just the dahlias. The zinnias come in yellow, pink-orange, and white."

"I'll bet they'll be good for drawing the butterflies too. What's going to be put in over there?" Ivy Mae pointed to an adjacent bed farther down the walk.

"Norman's in charge of putting in a few birdbaths over there."

Ivy Mae walked down the sidewalk for a better look. Two birdbaths stood on the sidewalk waiting to be installed. "Oh, that's going to look beautiful there. Where are you going to put the second one?"

Norman lifted off his cap and wiped his forehead. "Well, I'm thinking about right over there. I think it'd look good in front of the hydrangeas."

Ivy Mae surveyed the surrounding area. "What would you think of putting the blue one over here in this bed. You've got this beautiful yellow forsythia. Wouldn't it look lovely with a birdbath in front of it, especially since you have a bench over there? Maybe some irises on each side."

"She's got a point Norman." Ruby stood behind Ivy Mae looking the scene over.

"I can put it wherever you want it," Norman said. "As

long as you don't make me move it once it's in place. Let me get my shovel."

He came back shortly, shovel in hand. "I'm going to need to level the land up there a bit."

"Anything I can help you with?" Ivy Mae asked.

"I think I'm going to need a rake. We need to get this spot leveled and then we'll get the birdbath in place. I'll be right back."

"How about I start leveling for you?" Ivy Mae picked up the shovel and began to even up the ground, skimming a little dirt from one place to the other.

"How are you doing? Need some help?" Iris asked.

"Sure, go ahead. I wouldn't want you to feel deprived." Ivy Mae forked over the shovel to her sister.

She dug the shovel a little deeper into the dirt revealing the tip of a red cloth. The next shovel of dirt revealed even more of the cloth.

"Think you found some buried treasure there." Ivy Mae knelt down brushing away some dirt from the cloth. She had seen this before or something like it before. But where? She racked her brain, trying to remember.

"Sure looks like something is buried there," Iris said. She turned to see Norman coming up behind them, pushing a wheelbarrow full of pebbles and a rake.

Ivy Mae tugged the bundle out of the dirt. Then it hit her. This was the same kind of handkerchief that Charlie had given to Iris the day of the car accident. Could he own another one just like it? A sinking feeling hit Ivy Mae in the pit of her stomach as the pieces of the puzzle snapped into place. She didn't even have to unwrap the item in her hand to realize what it was. Still, she flipped the fabric aside.

Norman gasped at what he saw before him. A gun lay in Ivy Mae's hand. Norman sagged to his knees beside the ladies, his eyes were round and his hands began to shake. "That's my gun."

"Oh, my goodness," Ruby gasped. She was standing behind Norman staring at the weapon.

"I...I reported it stolen. I don't even know when it was stolen. I was going to do a routine cleaning on it the other day and it was just gone."

Iris looked around at everyone. "Don't you think we need to call the sheriff?" She stood up and backed away.

"Why is my gun buried here? Norman stammered.

The sound of footsteps behind them caught their attention and everyone turned to see Charlie. His gaze locked on the gun laying on the cloth. His eyes shot to his uncle, then each of the ladies. Sweat popped out on his forehead. He turned as if to run until Ivy Mae called out.

"Charlie, stop."

He turned around hesitantly. Ivy Mae felt her heart pounding in her chest. She saw Iris out of the corner of her eye. Her sister's face was pale. She took several slow steps back, reaching into her pocket. Ivy Mae hoped she was reaching for her phone.

Ivy Mae's voice grew stronger as she spoke. "You killed Justin, didn't you?" Charlie remained silent as the older woman spoke, her voice soft and soothing. "You did it for Cora didn't you? I've seen the way you look at her. You believed if you killed Justin, then the condo project would die in its tracks. Although she might never know, you could be her hero."

Charlie spun in his tracks racing down the sidewalk. Ivy Mae grabbed a shovel and slid it down the sidewalk, hitting Charlie in the back of one foot. He stumbled but didn't go down. Suddenly, something dark jutted out, caught his ankle, and sent him sprawling.

About that time the sounds of a siren could be heard from the front of the botanical gardens. Arthur unhooked his umbrella handle from Charlie's ankle and settled himself back on his bench, keeping a sharp eye on his prey.

Charlie sat up, hate radiating from his eyes. He looked at Ivy Mae, his words thick with emotion. "I did it for Cora and my uncle. I'd do anything for those two. Why couldn't you just leave this alone?" He started to stand.

"Stay put son. It's over." Arthur urged the boy.

"It's not over!" Charlie stood to sprint down the walk. Arthur whacked him in the back with his umbrella. Charlie turned glaring at the older man and started to run down the sidewalk again, straight into the substantial form of Sheriff McGuire. Charlie bounced off the man, falling to the sidewalk.

"Cuff him, Randall."

The deputy reached down and snapped the handcuffs on Charlie. Ivy Mae looked over at Norman. The hurt and anger were clearly visible on his face. Randall got Charlie to his feet and started to walk him back to the patrol car.

Veins throbbed on the sides of Norman's forehead. "I took you in. I gave you a second chance and what did you do?"

"He was poisoning your roses!" Spit flew from Charlie's mouth. "He wanted the extra section of land that the roses were on." His shoulder's sagged, "I spotted him one night back here, sprinkling something on them. And then Cora, she's so beautiful and so passionate about stopping those condos. I just couldn't let that scum win. I followed him that night. I knew he'd be back here." Charlie shrugged, "So I took care of the problem. You should be proud of me uncle."

Sheriff McGuire looked from Charlie to Norman. "Take him away, Randall."

CHAPTER TWENTY-THREE

"I'M glad everyone could come over tonight," Sara looked around as she came in came into the dining room from the kitchen.

Iris stood in the dining room with just some of the friends she made since she moved back to Blue Water Bay. They were spending the evening at Sara's. The table was full of everyone's favorite potluck dishes. Noah, Zoey, Ruby, and Arthur joined Sara, Ivy Mae, and Iris tonight.

"Alright everyone, I think we have everything ready. Why don't we sit down?"

They each took their seat around the old family table. Iris tapped her butter knife against the side of her water glass. "If I can just say a quick word. Even though I have visited Blue Water Bay on several occasions, now I'm happy to call it my home. I have also enjoyed meeting all of you. My sister has some wonderful friends and I'm happy to call you my friends too.

Ivy Mae reached over and squeezed her sister's hand. "And I'm ever so happy to have you here.

"We all are," Sara said.

They passed serving bowls around the table. Their plates were soon filled with portions of lasagna, glazed meatballs, deviled eggs, corn on the cob, zesty three-bean salad, and cheesy cornbread.

Noah looked across the table. "I heard stories of what happened the other day at the botanical garden. But I'm curious Ivy Mae, did I hear right? You caught Justin's killer?"

"Yes, she did," Ruby said. "You should have seen it."

"I wish I had."

"I heard you knocked Charlie down with a shovel. Is that true?" Zoey asked.

"Not quite," Ivy Mae admitted. "In fact, if it hadn't been for Arthur here, he may have actually gotten away. He's the real hero."

Arthur chuckled, "I don't know about that. My umbrella and I were just in the right place at the right time. That's all."

Iris looked over at Arthur. "How's your shoulder. It's a wonder he didn't pull it out of the socket."

"It's not doing too bad," Arthur rubbed his right shoulder.

"What are you talking about?" Zoey asked, looking back and forth between Iris and Arthur.

"You should have seen it. Charlie was running down the sidewalk and all of a sudden Arthur stuck his umbrella out and caught Charlie by the ankle." Ivy Mae threw her hands up in the air, "And boom, down he went. It was quite impressive."

"It was nothing," Arthur said, waving her comment away.

Ruby scooped a few more meatballs onto her plate. "I'm just concerned about Norman. He knew Charlie was troubled when he took him in, but I still feel bad for him."

"That's got to be rough," Iris said.

About that time there was a knock at the front door. Sara, hopped up heading to the door.

"I hope I'm not interrupting."

"Of course not, come on it," Sara responded.

"I was on my way to see your aunts when I spotted Ivy Mae's car here."

Sara walked the sheriff into the dining room.

"Oh, I'm sorry. I sure didn't mean to interrupt your dinner party."

"Nonsense Sheriff. You're just in time," Ivy Mae said.

"Yes, please have a seat," Iris added.

Sara came back into the dining room with a plate and silverware. "Here you go. Help yourself, as you can see, we have plenty."

"Well thank you. Don't mind if I do." After he had his plate loaded, he looked over at the sisters. "I was on my way over to talk to you."

"Oh? You have news about Charlie?"

Sheriff McGuire glanced around the table before continuing on. "I suppose this will make the papers soon enough. Yes, Charlie admitted to shooting Justin with his uncles' weapon. The white powder was indeed an herbicide. Charlie said Justin admitted to him that he was poisoning the roses. Seems like Justin thought if they died, then maybe the botanical garden would be inclined to sell the land that was being developed for the rose garden."

"And he did this all because of Cora?" Iris asked.

"Seems he was quite obsessed with her and he would do anything he thought would ...well make her happy. It's craziness," the sheriff said scooping himself some meatballs.

"Charlie also admitted to throwing that rock through your front window. He also said something about leaving a threatening note on your door. That puzzled me because I never heard about it. Did he do that?"

"Yes, he did," Iris answered. "Don't take it personally sheriff, Ivy Mae didn't even show it to me until the next day."

"I'll bet that was him in your yard that night," Noah said while snagging another piece of cornbread.

"And how come I didn't know about all this?" the sheriff huffed.

Ivy Mae held her hands up in front of her, "What? You don't really want me to call you about every little noise I hear, do you? We called when we really had something to report." Her clear laughter rang out, "You've got to have some nights off."

Hearty laughter rang out from the sheriff. "Well, I appreciate you thinking about me. Oh, I almost forgot, the reason I stopped by in the first place. Iris, I ran into Travis today over at the body shop. He said your car would be ready in just a day or two."

"Thanks, Sheriff I appreciate the info."

"Do you think you even need that car anymore since you have your tricycle?" Sara teased her aunt.

"Yes, I definitely want to keep my car, thank you." Iris paused, "Although I will say, I've grown accustomed to riding my tricycle. I actually rather like it."

Ivy Mae's head popped up. "Maybe we should start a bike club."

This brought a round of laughs from those sitting at the table.

"What? I think it's a great idea."

The sounds of silverware and bubbly voices rang throughout the room.

Iris looked around the table contentedly. She was home and happy to be there.

THE END

COMING SOON: VIOLETS ARE CLUES - A TWIN SISTERS COZY MYSTERY - BOOK 2

CHAPTER 1

"How are you doing with that lime zest?"

"Frankly I think my arm is going to fall off. Ha! These old elbows aren't what they used to be," Ivy Mae said as she scraped the tiny curls of lime zest into a bowl.

Patty looked over at Ivy Mae, wiping her hands on a nearby cloth. "Here, you come over here and stir this pot and I'll zest.

The ladies swapped spots in the shiny stainless-steel kitchen of The Fudgery. Patty was the owner of the little fudge shop, located on Main Street in the little town of Blue Water Bay. The shop boasted a red and white canopy out front and glass front cases inside, holding rich delectable stacks of fudge. Dark chocolate, creamy milk chocolate with and without pecans, white chocolate with hazelnuts, green striped mint fudge, peanut butter fudge stacked next to the kid's favorite cookies and cream fudge and cake batter fudge dotted with sprinkles.

"Thanks for coming in to help me, this morning. I'm

anxious to see how this recipe turns out. You know, I always try to come up with a couple of new flavors before the summer tourist season gets into full swing. I feel like I'm starting a little late this year."

"Oh, you'll be fine. I mean, this recipe sounds amazing. Whoever would have thought to make Key Lime fudge."

"Oh, lots of people, I'm sure," Patty grinned at her friend. "I'm almost finished here." A moment later the timer dinged and Ivy Mae pulled the bubbling pot off the burner. "Be careful, this is really hot," Ivy Mae cautioned needlessly.

"Now for the good stuff." Patty stirred in the white chocolate and marshmallows, while Ivy Mae added the lime zest and lime juice.

"Oh my goodness, take a whiff of that." The fragrance of lime filled the little kitchen. "I can't wait to try this," Ivy Mae eyed the pot.

Patty laughed as she stirred, "Well be patient. You can have this pot after I scrap it out, just wait until it cools. You know that sugar is really hot."

The bell over the door rang as Patty poured the mixture into a prepared pan. "Keep working, I'll go help them."

As Ivy Mae exited the back, she spotted Ruby coming into the little shop.

Ruby inhaled, "Do I smell lime?" Her brown eyes sparkled with excitement. "I love lime."

"You smelled right. Patty's working on a new recipe."

"Well let her know, I'm available to taste test anytime she wants."

"I'll keep that in mind," Patty said coming out of the back room. "Good to see you Ruby. How's everything going down at the garden?"

Blue Water Bay was home to the Blackwater Botanical Garden where Ruby worked.

"Good overall, she paused. "Norman is trying to come to terms with the fact his nephew confessed to killing that guy."

Not too long ago the town had been divided over a proposed condominium complex that was going to be built between the botanical garden and the Willow Creek Wildlife Refuge. Tempers flared and the man who wanted to build the complex ended up dead, with his body left in the botanical garden. "Now everyone was gearing up for the Summer Spectacular, which is why I'm here today." She held out a pot of violets to Patty.

"I love this time of year," Patty said as she took the potted plant. She glanced around her shop, placing the plant on one side of the cash register. There was a plastic stick in the plant holding a small card advertising the Summer Spectacular.

Every year the botanical garden held a festival to promote the benefits of gardening, not to mention showing off their beautiful summer blossoms and raising money for the garden. This included passing out potted plants to the shop owners as part of the advertising.

"And that's why I'm working on two new recipes. I love having something that screams summer."

"So, what did you come up with this year? Lime something I'm sure, I can smell it."

Patty smiled, "Yes, I'm making a Key Lime Fudge and I think I'll try something with orange, but I haven't figured that one out yet."

"Sounds like a winner to me," Ruby said. "I can't wait to try them."

"Me too!" Ivy Mae wondered if the remnants in the pot in the back room had cooled enough to try.

Ruby turned, "You ladies have a good day and keep cooking. I've got to go deliver the rest of these violets."

"We'll see you later." Patty and Ivy Mae waved goodbye to her and returned to the kitchen. Ivy Mae grabbed a spoon and scraped remnants of the creamy lime goodness out of the pot. She closed her eyes, the tangy lime flavors exploding in her mouth.

"That is so good."

Patty grabbed her own spoon, scraping a little fudge out of the pot. She rolled the concoction around in her mouth, tasting the flavors. "Does it have enough lime?"

"Oh, yes. I think there's a good balance. Not too tangy, not too sweet."

"Good, now I'll start working on my ideas for my next creation. I haven't quite figured it out yet."

"Well, you do that and I'll clean up back here." After Patty headed back up front, Ivy Mae picked up her spoon again and happily scraped out all the limey fudge remnants she could from the pot. "Oh, my goodness that is so good," she said to herself. Ivy Mae finished cleaning the kitchen and turned to head back up front when she heard it. The wail of a siren pierced the peace and quiet. Even with the door to the shop closed the ladies could hear it.

"That sounds really close," Ivy Mae frowned as she started for the front door.

Patty was already headed to the door, "Yes it does, doesn't it?" She opened the door looking to the right and the left. "That's because it is."

Ivy Mae poked her head out the door and noticed a sheriff's car that pulled up in front of the business on the corner.

"Oh my, I hope everything's okay," Ivy Mae said watching closely.

Both Sheriff McGuire and one of his deputies hurried into the newly opened Zumba studio. Rousing music blared when they opened the door to the studio.

"What do you suppose is going on down there?" Ivy Mae continued to watch as Patty returned to the shop.

"No idea, but I can guess," Patty sighed.

"Oh?" Patty's comment had captured Ivy Mae's attention. She returned to the shop, the little bell tinkled in her wake. When Patty didn't elaborate, Ivy Mae spoke up. "Well don't hold back on me? What do you know?"

Patty shook her head and pressed her lips together not saying anything.

"Hello," Ivy Mae wasn't about to give up. "I know you're not going to ignore me."

Patty looked up, her hands on her hips, "I swear, you are worse than a dog with a bone. I'm going to start calling you Daisy."

Ivy Mae was the proud owner of a little canine fluff ball, named Daisy.

Ivy Mae's laughter rang out, filling the little shop. "I don't care what you call me if you keep me updated on town business."

"Oh, town business. That's what you're going to call it?" Patty shook her head. "Fine, I'll tell you. Just keep in mind, I haven't seen this for myself."

Ivy Mae waved a hand, urging her younger friend on.

"I hear that Victoria is not too happy with her new business neighbor, that's all."

"Wait, who's Victoria?"

"You know, Victoria Rivers, she owns the Seaside

Serenity Spa. It's right down the street, next door from the new Zumba studio."

"Huh, I thought I knew all the shop owners in the area. Guess I hadn't met her. I saw the new business on the corner, but hadn't really paid attention to what it was."

"Yes, it's an exercise studio, specializing in Zumba."

"Sounds alright to me. So what's the problem? Do the two owners not get along?"

"Well from what I've heard, Victoria got into it with Nicole. Nicole Blakeman is the owner of the new Zumba studio."

"Seems like they would actually make a good partnership. Exercise at the Zumba studio, then treat yourself to a massage next door," Ivy Mae said.

"You would think, but the problem is the sound from the Zumba studio. Nicole likes to crank up the music when she has her classes. Well, you could imagine, the sounds of the music from her classes interrupts the peace and quiet in the spa."

"Oh!" Ivy Mae's eyes were wide. I can see the problem there."

Patty cocked her head to the side. "Can you imagine going in for a massage and having music blaring away? There goes your restful calming massage."

"That could be a problem. But surely they can come to a resolution."

"I'm sure hope they can. I mean really, they're adults after all."

NOTES FROM THE AUTHOR

Thank you so much for reading the first book in this new series, *A Twin Sisters Cozy Mystery*. I have enjoyed writing these stories and watching my characters develop over the course of these books. I hope you will enjoy them.

All four books in this series includes:

Roses Are Dead
Violets Are Clues
Sugar Is Deceit
You Are Due

If you have liked this series, you might like my other series, you can find them on Amazon here: A Copper Ridge Mystery (10 book series)

If you would like to receive my newsletter and get information on future books, please go to my website at www.amygrundy.com

Again, thank you for reading this book, I sincerely hope you enjoyed it.

ABOUT THE AUTHOR

Hello readers.

My name is Amy and I'm the author of "A Copper Ridge Mystery" series and "A Twin Sisters Cozy Mystery" series. I'd like to say I've had a passion for writing my whole life, but that would be untrue. My husband of forty plus years encouraged me to try my hand at writing cozy mysteries in the spring of 2019 and I LOVE IT!

A former nurse, I live in the Houston area. I enjoy a quiet life with my husband, children, and grandchildren. My family also includes one lovable dog and four very independent cats. When I'm not writing I enjoy running marathons with support from my friends, jigsaw puzzles and always a good cup of coffee.

I hope you will enjoy my books and thank you for your support.

Made in the USA
Las Vegas, NV
30 April 2022